50831375

C000040959

TOUGH IN THE SADDLE

Todhunter Ballard was born in Cleveland, Ohio. He also wrote under the name **Parker Bonner**. He graduated with a Bachelor's degree from Wilmington College in Ohio, having majored in mechanical engineering. His early years were spent working as an engineer before he began writing fiction for the magazine market. As W. T. Ballard he was one of the regular contributors to *Black Mask Magazine* along with Dashiell Hammett and Erle Stanley Gardner. Although Ballard published his first Western story in *Cowboy Stories* in 1936, the same year he married Phoebe Dwiggins, it wasn't until *Two-Edged Vengeance* (1951) that he produced his first Western novel. Ballard later claimed that Phoebe, following their marriage, had co-written most of his fiction with him, and perhaps this explains, in part, his memorable female characters. Ballard's Golden Age as a Western author came in the 1950s and extended to the early 1970s. *Incident at Sun Mountain* (1952), *West of Quarantine* (1953), and *High Iron* (1953) are among his finest early historical titles, published by Houghton Mifflin. After numerous traditional Westerns for various publishers, Ballard returned to the historical novel in *Gold in California!* (1965) which earned him a Golden Spur Award from the Western Writers of America. It is a story set during the Gold Rush era of the 'Forty-Niners. However, an even more panoramic view of that same era is to be found in Ballard's *magnum opus*, *The Californian* (1971), with its contrasts between the *Californios* and the emigrant gold-seekers, and the building of a freight line to compete with Wells Fargo. It was in his historical fiction that Ballard made full use of his background in engineering combined with exhaustive historical research. However, these novels are also character-driven, gripping a reader from first page to last with their inherent drama and the spirit of adventure so true of those times.

TOUGH IN THE SADDLE

Parker Bonner

GUNSMOKE

First published in the US by Monarch Books

This hardback edition 2013
by AudioGO Ltd
by arrangement with
Golden West Literary Agency

ISBN 978 1 471 32151 1

British Library Cataloguing in Publication Data available.

Printed and bound in Great Britain by
TJ International Limited

CHAPTER ONE

BOYD REYNOLDS felt a deep sense of homecoming as, at sunset, he brought his tired horse down the zigzag trail out of the Crossing's main street.

True, the ranch still lay far ahead, in the rolling meadows of Hunt Valley, but Alf Bentley's store was a sort of milepost, a familiar beacon from his childhood.

He had ridden here often, for though the store had always been headquarters for the hill outlaws, Reynolds had been recognized as one whom they need not fear. He expected no trouble now. Four years changed little in this country.

At one time the Crossing had been a town of considerable size. It stood in the high canyon of the Hunt River, five miles above the mouth where the wild stream broke from its narrow defile into the wide valley. The single street, once crowded with supply wagons, with ore carts, with two thousand people, was now nothing but a grass-grown track twisting between the crumbling ruins of the fifty or so buildings that remained.

For the Bentley mine, which had been the sole excuse for the town's existence, had flooded twenty years before. The miners and merchants and sharpers who had swelled its population had drifted away until Alf Bentley himself was the Crossing's single inhabitant.

The headframe, the dump and the rusting mill stood like ghosts on the canyon wall above, silent reminders that this desolate spot had once produced over a million dollars in gold.

There was a light in the store, and toward this Boyd Reynolds urged his horse. Once it had been the town's hotel, with an impressive lobby, an ornate bar, and card games that ran around the clock. But for years now it had sold staples, hardware and rope, filling the simple needs of the brush jumpers and wanted men who sought refuge in the lonely cabins and rickety shacks hidden in the barren folds of the stone hills.

It was a lonely place, shunned by the citizens of Kernville and the lush acres that stretched away around it, but Boyd had spent many hours here and in the grim hills that rose in increasing emptiness toward the west.

Even as a child he had had a fiddle foot, a bottomless curiosity that had sent him up each new trail he found. In the last four years it had sent him across the full breadth of the West, from the tree-shrouded coasts of Oregon and northern California, to the table-level plains of the Texas gulf coast.

Now it had brought him full circle, and as his horse's hoofs crushed the tall grass of the track, he smiled. He and Alf Bentley had shared a sense of close companionship.

They were as different as men can be. Boyd was big, with a powerfully muscular body kept taut by much hard riding, young, with the world beckoning him.

Bentley was middle-aged, a short man with a totally bald head, a hairless face, pug nose and rosebud mouth. He should have been embittered, since he had squandered all of the wealth his father had wrested from the mine, in vain efforts to drain it, to reach the rich ore that he was certain lay at the lower levels beneath the waters which filled the shafts, the crosscuts and the stopes.

But his optimism was boundless. Every time Boyd had visited the Crossing, Bentley had had a new plan to reopen the mine and revive the town, and as he swung the horse in at the rotting rail and stepped down, the curve of his rather thin lips widened in anticipation. Bentley surely would greet him with some grandiose scheme, a new way to drive a tunnel from the mountain's foot, five miles through county rock, to draw off the evil waters from the old workings.

He turned, glancing up and down the street, surprised that there was not a single horse in sight. In the days before he had ridden out, the gaunt hill people had been wont to gather here by twos and threes, to sit and gossip idly on the wide porch, to lean against the elaborate bar or play a little desultory poker for phantom stakes.

6

He mounted the porch then, moving easily toward the door which in other days had been the bar entrance. He reached the solid panel and thrust it open, expecting to see Alf Bentley perched on the high stool at the far end of the bar, which he used as a kind of throne.

The stool was empty, but the room was not. He was surprised to see three men ranged along the bar, since there were no horses at the rail. He swung slowly and discovered three more at a poker table in the rear corner.

He stopped. Behind him the door's latch clicked. He turned back quietly, to find himself facing four other men, and none of them could he remember having ever seen before.

One, a step forward of the others, was very tall, very thin, holding a heavy gun in his hand, its ugly muzzle steady on the buckle of Boyd's belt.

"He's alone." The man had a high, nasal voice.

A heavy-set man with thick shoulders and long, dangling arms came away from the bar, walking forward on legs which seemed not to bend.

"Get his horse off the street."

Boyd twisted slowly. His eyes, usually open and candid and inclined to smile, looked now like sheets of gray steel. His tone was low, unhurried.

"Will someone tell me what this is all about? Where's Alf Bentley?"

"He ain't here."

"And who are you?"

The heavy man eyed him boldly, his manner assured, as one who knows that the game is entirely in his hands.

"I might ask you that, but I won't bother. Whatever name you used wouldn't be important. What matters is that you had the idiocy to ride up here by yourself to spy, or didn't Jud Laws tell you this is out of bounds for TC men?"

"What's Jud Laws got to do with it?"

"Next you'll tell me you don't even know him."

"I know him. I haven't seen him in years."

The man's mouth split open in a red, ugly grin. "Now you'll say you never heard of the TC, huh?"

"Of course I've heard of TC. What about it?"

7

A man came in through the door behind Reynolds, saying, "The horse has a brand I never saw before. It isn't TC."

Reynolds turned to look at him coldly. "I bought it in Denver."

"Laws bringing in some new blood, huh? How long you been working for TC?"

"I never worked for TC in my life."

"Then what are you doing here?"

"I rode in to see Alf Bentley. I've been away four years. I own the Running R, down in the valley."

There was a burst of laughter throughout the room. The apelike man said, "The TC owns the Running R—and everything else in the valley."

Boyd Reynolds felt his big body tighten. "You're crazy. My father started Running R forty years ago when he came up the trail with Charles Goodnight."

The tall, slim man snickered. "He's gonna claim his name is Reynolds."

"It is."

The answer brought further jeering laughter. The short man leaned with derisive languor against the bar.

"Great story, fella. Hugh Reynolds was shot off his horse two years back."

Boyd Reynolds started visibly, then hid his consternation and said calmly, "I'm his younger brother, Boyd."

"He was killed in San Francisco the year after he left here. You'll have to do better than that, stranger. Jud Laws has coached you pretty good, but not good enough. What are you doing up this canyon? What's Laws trying to pull now?"

"I tell you I don't know anything about all of this."

"Get his gun, Slim."

The muscles along Boyd Reynolds' jaw line bunched. No one had ever taken his gun from him. He stood quiet while the tall man lifted the heavy weapon from the sagging holster and stepped back. The short man, apparently the leader, turned to the room.

"Now what do we do with him?"

"Shoot him," said Slim. "Shoot him or hang him, it's all one to me."

The others nodded, uncaring. The method mattered not to them, so long as he died. Boyd Reynolds had a sudden falling sensation at the pit of his stomach. He had never been truly afraid before, but he was thoroughly frightened now. These men were not joking; this was not some heavy-handed ribbing. They meant exactly what they said. He sensed that they would destroy him with no more compunction than they would have in killing a rattlesnake.

"Hold on a minute," he said, managing to keep his voice steady. "If I'm going to die I'd at least like to know why."

Slim growled in his throat. "You don't need to be told, stupid. You know, all right."

"Suppose I don't? Suppose you're making a mistake?"

A fierceness rose in Slim's high voice. "Some of your boys killed my brother the day before yesterday. You were a damn fool to ride in here. Now, how do you want it, a gun or a rope?"

Reynolds said evenly, "A gun."

"All right, walk out into the street. I'll count ten, then you start running."

"To hell with that. Get it over with."

They faced each other, Reynolds' eyes hard on the other's. The man shrugged.

"Okay, if that's how you want it." His hand dropped and lifted his big gun from his holster.

A voice near the door whispered suddenly, "Wait!"

Slim checked the upward swing of the muzzle, for the sound of a horse being ridden up the rocky street came plainly into the room.

The short man lifted a hand for silence. "See who it is."

The man who had whispered, cracked the door, peering cautiously through the narrow slot. The sun was gone, but the street outside was still filled with twilight.

The silence ran on until Reynolds thought his chest would burst with tension. Then the watcher turned back.

"It's all right. It's Alf."

Boyd Reynolds felt a weakness flood through him, a rush of relief. He knew he would never come closer to death than he had this evening until life finally deserted his body.

Then he jerked taut again, for Slim was saying, "Might as well finish this," and again bringing up his gun.

"No." Boyd Reynolds knew his voice was almost a croak, and he fought to control it. "Just a minute. Alf knows me. Alf can tell you you're wrong."

Slim did hesitate. The short man shrugged. "Might as well wait. Alf will be here in a second."

Boyd, who had almost stopped breathing, slowly filled his lungs.

He heard Bentley's boots on the porch and saw the men before him split to let Alf pass. Then he was staring into the mine owner's face.

Bentley had not changed greatly in the intervening years, but Boyd knew that he himself had. He had been barely twenty when he had had his last fight with Hugh, had climbed on his horse, swearing he would never enter Colorado again. At the time he had weighed not over a hundred and forty pounds. Now he would tip the beam at a good one-eighty. His body had filled out, his face had lost its boyish, narrow uncertainty and become gaunt and solid.

He read no recognition in the fat man's face as Bentley stopped to scrutinize him.

"Who's this?"

Slim's wolfish grin sliced his face and the gun tipped up once more. "He claims you know him."

"Alf," Boyd said, "Look at me. It's Boyd Reynolds. 'Kid' Reynolds. Don't you remember?'

The fat man's face puckered in a tight frown. He stood for a long moment, and gradually his eyes changed, becoming uncertain.

"You do look like the Kid." He said it slowly, then shook his head in indecision. "But Boyd's dead."

A great bursting impatience filled Boyd. "You old mountain goat. I'm no more dead than you are, although I would have been in another minute if you hadn't showed up. Remember the rainy day we took thirteen trout out of the potholes? Remember the ledge we found back of Antelope Seep? Remember the time Lizzy Cowan slapped your face at the Whiteside dance?"

"Damn it, it is Boyd." The fat man took a sudden step forward and threw his arms around the younger man.

For all his short stature, for all his flesh, Bentley was one of the most powerful men Boyd had ever met. He felt himself lifted clear of the floor, swung around as if he were weightless, and perched on the end of the bar.

Then Bentley stepped back to examine him better. "If you're alive, how come the San Francisco police sent your watch and things to Hugh? They found letters from him in your pocket."

Boyd looked startled, then he said quickly, "That's easy to explain. I got rolled one night. I'd been playing poker in a Barbary Coast saloon, and drinking a lot. When I left the place a couple of toughs jumped me. We had quite a fight before they knocked me cold. When I came to, I was in an alley. They'd taken my coat and vest, my money and my gun. I suppose one of them must have been wearing my coat and got himself killed, and the police mistook his body for mine."

The men had formed a tight group around him and Boyd sensed that they were still suspicious.

Slim said, "Didn't you report the robbery to the police?"

Boyd shook his head. "Why? I'd been down on the Coast where no man in his right mind goes. There are fifty robberies in San Francisco every night, to say nothing of a couple of murders. I figured I was lucky to be alive. I went down to the docks and got a job."

Alf Bentley said, "When Hugh heard you were dead it pretty well broke him up. Maybe if he'd known you were alive it would have been different."

"How, different?" Boyd looked around at the watching faces. "Someone said that Hugh is dead. I nearly got killed a few minutes ago. What's going on around here?"

"Murder," said Alf Bentley. "Cold-blooded murder. There's no other word for it. Come on, have a drink and I'll tell you about it."

11

CHAPTER TWO

SILENTLY the men lined up along the ornate counter. The fancy back-bar which had once held rows of elaborate bottles was now stacked with coils of rope, boxes of ammunition, and a hundred other items which served as the bulk of Alf's trade stock.

The proud mirror which had been freighted all the way from Denver in a special wagon was cracked and splotched where the silver backing had peeled away.

The liquor bottles had vanished, replaced by a small keg sitting on the end of the bar. Some of the crystal glasses, once in common use at the Bentley House, remained, lined along the high shelf above the mirror. Alf brought them down one at a time, making a ritual of the act. He used a gray bar-rag to wipe out the dust, then filled them from the keg, passing them along the bar from hand to hand until each man had a drink.

"Here's to you, Kid." His voice held a quaver of real emotion. "It's like rolling back the clock to see you standing there. You look a lot like your daddy, and those were better days. I guess we'll never see their like again."

This was so unlike Bentley that Boyd stared at the fat man. Alf had always been the last to give up on anything. He drank the raw liquor, feeling it warm his tired body and near-empty stomach. Then he set the glass on the bar.

"All right. What's happened in Hunt Valley?"

"Jud Laws," said Bentley, and in a sudden flash of temper hurled his empty glass the length of the room to crash into a thousand pieces, spintering against the rear wall. "Damn him."

"Jud Laws?" Boyd remembered Jud Laws well, if not favorably. Laws had been the pint-sized son of a small rancher. He had been a sneak, a carrier of tales. He had gotten Boyd and the rest of the school in trouble a dozen

12

times. He was, to Boyd's mind, as useless a man as existed. "What about Jud Laws?"

Alf Bentley blew out his breath. "Jud got a job with Transcontinental Cattle Company right after you went away. Somehow he got around Parkhurst, you remember him, that Englishman who was manager."

Boyd remembered him vaguely. He had never paid much attention to Parkhurst, or to the English capitalists who had bought the old Hunt ranch. He had been too busy having a good time to pay much attention to anything.

Bentley was refilling the glasses. He redistributed them before saying, "It took Jud just six months to con the Englishman into making him foreman. Then Parkhurst fell off the canyon wall and broke his neck. And Jud became manager. Imagine that little pipsqueak being manager of the biggest ranch in the valley."

Boyd could not.

"But it still wasn't big enough for him." Bentley's voice had grown bitter. "Right away he began to squeeze the smaller outfits, paying off old grudges, you might think. Some got tired of the fight and sold out. Some got loans at the bank and were foreclosed. The TC bought them up at the sheriff's sales."

Boyd was watching him intently, his face without expression. "What happened to my brother? What happened to the Running R?"

"Hugh was shot off the side porch." The words were flat, final.

In spite of himself, Boyd Reynolds winced. Then he said in a controlled voice, "And the ranch?"

"It was mortgaged. The TC bought it in. They were the only bidder."

For a long minute there was complete silence in the old room. Finally Boyd said, "So Jud has the whole valley. His English bosses should be very happy with him."

A sour laugh ran along the bar, a wicked sound, without a trace of humor.

Bentley grunted. "The TC is going broke."

"Broke?"

Bentley's rosebud mouth looked redder than ever as he

13

pursed his lips. "That's the story we hear. The way Jud tells it, a lot of the ranch stock winter-killed in the deep snow last year. The rest is being rustled, right and left."

"Rustled by whom?"

Again Bentley indicated the bar. "By the men in this room. It isn't true. The boys may have taken a stray now and then for food, but what would they do with stolen beef on the hoof? You can't drive cattle up through the badlands behind here, and certainly no one but Jud's men are going to be allowed to drive anything out the other end of the valley."

Reynolds' eyes were narrow. "What's that supposed to mean, Alf?"

"Form your own opinion, Kid. There's a rumor of a new spread being set up in North Park. We heard Jud Laws has an interest in it, that maybe he owns the whole thing. The word is, they're running a lot of cows that once carried the TC and other brands that Jud bought up down here."

"I see."

"Not all of it, you don't. The Britishers wrote to the governor that they were being robbed. The governor appointed a special commissioner from the attorney general's office to investigate. He's in the valley now. He went to the local sheriff and the county attorney. Both of them are in Jud's pay. They put the blame on us hill people, and we've been ordered to clear out of the state."

"Oh? When was this?"

"A week ago. They caught Slim's brother and Howard Hayes over on Cow Creek, day before yesterday, and hung them both."

Reynolds turned and looked at the slender man. "Seems to me, if that's so, even Jud Laws wouldn't be fool enough to send a single rider in here. What made you think I was his spy?"

Slim said, "Decoy maybe, while they sneak up on us." He glanced at Bentley.

Bentley nodded. "We're expecting a visit. So if you're smart, Boyd, you'll turn around and ride out. They're trying to make the hills too hot for any of us. There's no call for you to get mixed up in it."

14

Boyd Reynolds leaned closer against the bar. "You have that poor an opinion of me, Alf?"

Bentley's tone held apology. "Well, you were always a fiddle-footed young'un."

"I was a kid." Reynolds was thinking aloud as much as talking to the fat man. "I had nothing to fight for. Hugh was running the ranch. If I'd stayed I'd have had no say in it. But now—"

"Now you haven't got a ranch. None of us has anything. Jud has sworn to run us out or hang us to the nearest tree, and he's got thirty or forty men to make it stick."

"I'm not convinced I haven't got a ranch."

They stared at him. Slim laughed harshly.

"You just try riding up to the Running R and see how long you last. Jud is using it for his northern line camp. He's got at least ten men there."

Bentley was shaking his head like a metronome. "You haven't got a chance, Kid. The law says the bank foreclosed and sold your spread under the sheriff's hammer. That kind of deed takes precedence over any other. I should know the law," he said with a bitter, short laugh. "Lawyers cost me enough, all the years I been trying to hold my mine."

Boyd's jaw set firmly. "I don't claim to know law, but I own half the Running R. I certainly signed no mortgage, nor received any bank loan. As far as I'm concerned, the bank made a bad loan."

"But you were dead."

"I'm not dead." He smiled very faintly. "As I trust that Jud may soon find out."

There were sniggers among the men, then Bentley began to chuckle.

"I'd sure like to see his face when he learns you're alive. But you won't make it. He has all the law in the territory behind him, even the judge."

"That's to be seen."

"And even if you win back the land, what are you going to do for cattle?"

"The record of the sale will show how many the bank turned over to TC. I will collect that number."

"By yourself?"

Boyd looked speculatively around the room, but before he could speak, the door burst open and a boy of perhaps fourteen ran in.

"They're coming."

At once the room galvanized into action. Men snatched up rifles from where they had left them against the walls, and raced for the rear door. Within three minutes Boyd and Alf Bentley were alone in the old saloon.

"Your visitors?"

Bentley nodded grimly. "The TC. They sent word we had until tonight to clear out of the hills, that they were going to burn the town and ride down every man still around."

"But you stayed."

"You didn't think I'd high-tail?" The fat man sounded offended. "This is my home."

"Still, the rest ran."

"Don't bet on it." Alf Bentley grinned, and a new life seemed to fill him. "TC is apt to find it harder to ride out of here than to ride in."

"A trap?"

"And I'm the bait." The fat man found the idea amusing. "If it was dark and deserted in here they'd come in easy. Now they've seen the light. I wish we'd moved your horse. They'll wonder who it belongs to."

"To me."

"You'd better duck out of here, boy."

Reynolds said softly, "If I'm going to fight TC I may as well start now. Let's get those extra glasses out of sight. Then we can have a quiet drink."

They were at the bar when the rush of horses whispered along the grass-grown street. Reynolds tried to guess the number of men from the volume of sound, and failed.

Bentley stood behind his bar, a shotgun on the shelf beneath its high top. Reynolds faced him, his back to the door.

He heard the horses pull up, heard the harsh commands to watch the street, to check the horse at the rail, then the stamp of feet as three men mounted the porch. The door slammed open.

Without turning he looked up into the cracked mirror.

A big man stood in the lead, a man taller than Reynolds by a good inch, heavy in the shoulders. He stopped, framed in the doorway, his light eyes raking the room. His hair was long, curling beneath the band of his bell-crowned hat, looking golden in the light from the old crystal chandelier.

He came on into the room, trailed by two men, each carrying a rifle. Bentley put down his glass slowly. He stood, his big belly pressed against the inner rim of the bar top, both hands out of sight. Reynolds knew that they folded around the twin-barreled shotgun.

"Watch those door hinges, Cleaver. They aren't as new as they once were." His voice showed no emotion. He might have been remarking on the weather.

The big blond moved forward. There was an arrogance about him that needed no words to tell his contempt.

"You were told to get out, fat man."

"This is my home." There was a dignity in Bentley which Reynolds had never before recognized. "I was born here, Cleaver, and here I die."

"You likely will," the big man said, and one of his henchmen laughed. "We're going to burn this place, old man, and burn everything that's left of this rotting town. You had your chance. You didn't take it."

Bentley said nothing and Cleaver turned his attention to Reynolds, who had wheeled around slowly, putting his elbows on the bar.

"That your horse out there?"

Reynolds still held a half-filled whiskey glass in his hand. He raised it to his lips and tossed off the fiery liquid in a deliberately long throw.

"It is."

"Who are you? Where you from? What are you doing here?"

Reynolds reached back to set the empty glass on the counter. "Which question would you like answered first?"

His voice was even, unhurried, but rising within him was a savage wrath. He had never liked arrogant men; he had despised bullies all of his life, and Cleaver was both.

The fact that any man dared to challenge his right to come and go would have been enough, but added to this

17

was the knowledge that this giant represented the TC, represented Jud Laws, and the possibility that this might well be the man who had shot his brother down.

"Damnit," said Cleaver, and the raw edge of his temper showed in his eyes as well as in his voice. "Don't talk back to me. You're a stranger, so maybe you don't know what you're doing. I've never seen you around before. I never forget a face."

Reynolds made no answer.

"I don't know the brand your horse wears. If you're just a saddle bum drifting through, keep moving. You've got five minutes to ride out. But if I ever lay eyes on you in this country again, it will be the last day you live."

"You must be God," Boyd Reynolds told him. "I never heard that anyone had authority in these hills, not even the federal government."

His tone was mocking now, but his eyes were slate. He straightened away from the bar, bending a trifle forward so that his arm had room to sweep down for the holstered gun. While Cleaver still stood in a shocked stillness, Boyd went on:

"I don't think you are. And the man doesn't breathe who tells me where to ride, or when."

He waited. The figures behind Cleaver had made as if to raise their rifles, but in one smooth motion Alf Bentley swung the twin barrels of his shotgun into view, covering them. His voice was tight, inviting, almost pleading.

"Make me shoot. That's all I want. Make me shoot."

Cleaver said in a dry, husky tone, "I've got twenty men on the street, you old fool. Put that gun down."

The fat man laughed at him. "You're the fool. I've got men in every building in the Crossing. One shot and they'll cut loose. Think that over, Max Cleaver. You're in a box."

As if in confirmation of his words there was a high, wild yell from outside, then the sudden explosion of a dozen guns. The night, which had been as quiet as a forsaken cemetery, erupted into sudden, shrieking violence.

Cleaver's left guard lost his head. He brought up his rifle. The shotgun behind Reynolds roared and its double

18

charge struck the guard in the chest, nearly tearing him in two.

The shotgun's blast came so close to Reynolds' shoulder that he felt the wind of its passing. He threw himself sideways, going to one knee as Alf Bentley dropped behind the bar.

Cleaver had freed his gun in the same instant, and as he threw himself toward a table, Reynolds snapped a shot at him. He was shooting upward, at an angle. The bullet missed Cleaver but struck the swinging lamp, shattering it into a thousand pieces, casting the room into a quick, heavy darkness, spraying oil across the floor.

A small flame flickered, almost died, then caught, flared up from tinder-dry wood.

Reynolds snapped another shot at the place where he had last seen Cleaver. This, too, missed, but hit the man behind him. In the new light of the little flame Reynolds saw him spin and pitch forward. From the street outside, guns continued to hammer, and the night was hideous with their thunder.

Cleaver yelled. No one could tell what he said. In a crawling dive he flung himself through the door to the semidarkness of the street.

The fat man was around the bar, moving faster than Boyd thought possible, stamping at the licking tongue of flame as it raced across the floor from one oil splotch to the next. Reynolds joined him, but it was a losing fight. The old boards sucked at the liquid, and the fire bit into the splinters raised by a thousand boots.

The racing fire reached the wall and ran up the shards of drapes which hung there, as dry as autumn grass.

From the corner of his eye Reynolds saw the man he had shot drag himself up crookedly and stagger through the door. A bullet from the outside darkness knocked him to the dust.

The fat man gave up his frantic dance among the flames. "Get the ammunition out," he panted, running to sweep the boxed shells from the back-bar.

Reynolds spun, glancing around the reddening room. The man Bentley had shot lay sprawled in the middle of the

19

floor, flames licking at his blood-stained coat. Boyd leaped forward, caught him under the shoulders and hauled him into the night.

The TC crowd had remounted and were now milling in a slow retreat, still exchanging shots with the hill men whom they could not see, holed up as they were in the old buildings that lined the neglected thoroughfare.

Light blooming through the saloon's windows pierced the gloom with a sanguine glow, catching the routed riders in a brilliant, bloody bath, picking out Reynolds beside the door. A bullet struck the wall beside him and he dropped across the still figure he had dragged forth. There was no longer need to think of him. He was dead.

Alf Bentley came struggling out, his arms cradling all the shells he could carry. A bullet nicked his shoulder. He dropped his burden in the dust and howled, flinging to Reynolds' side as he hauled at his old-fashioned Colts. Then he was firing at the retreating horsemen as they tried to cover the withdrawal of their wounded.

Suddenly they were gone, vanishing around the curve of the canyon, the hoofs echoing as they clattered down the stony drop toward the mouth of the valley below.

Now the fire was spreading to the neighboring buildings, and the hill men scurried from their hiding places to lead their horses to safety. Bentley had quit firing and stood in the street, turning helplessly, staring around and around while his town went up in billowing smoke and raging flame.

The reaching fingers of fire created their own high wind, and, abetted by the draft of the canyon, streaked upward in a crackling, roaring frenzy as if ridden by the banshees. The rush of sound almost drowned the cries wrenched from the fat man.

"Damn them all! Damn Jud Laws and damn Max Cleaver and damn every other TC murderer. I'll kill them all!"

Reynolds ran up, catching his arm and piloting him in a staggering run for safety from the roasting heat. They joined the rest of the grim colony, bunched on the lee hillside, and stood waiting while the town was turned to ashes.

Two of their members were bleeding from flesh wounds, and Reynolds used the time helping to bandage them and

20

to investigate and bind up Bentley's shoulder. But at least, in a count of noses, none of the hill men had died.

They returned to the street as the ashes cooled. They found the bodies of Reynolds' and Bentley's victims, and one other TC man. They had no way of telling how many of the invaders were wounded, but three horses made silent mounds in the roadway.

"Well, we whipped them." It was Slim Maynard, speaking in a gusty sigh.

Reynolds said tightly, "Another victory like this and you'll all be dead. The Crossing is gone. That was your headquarters."

They looked at each other wordlessly.

"How about helping me to take back the Running R? If we stay together we'll be hard to beat. If we scatter, they can pick us off one by one."

Bentley's rage had run its course, and settled ino a cold inner core. He drew a long, ragged breath. "I'm with you. Anything you say, just so I get Jud Laws."

"Anybody else?" Reynolds' eyes ran over the shaken group.

There was a moment's hesitation, then Maynard spoke. "I'm in."

It was a signal. One after another now added his voice. Boyd Reynolds might not have a ranch, but because of this night he had a crew.

The smile with which he acknowledged each recruit held no humor, only the promise of a hard and bitter fight.

CHAPTER THREE

IT WAS IN THE LATE SEVENTIES when Luther Hunt, with a trail herd and twenty-five tough Texans, drove up from New Mexico to Pueblo. They swung northwest, crossed the South Platte above where the Hunt River emptied into the larger stream, and came into the empty valley.

For ten years he had been the region's driving force, gradually joined by a dozen other ranchers, of whom Boyd Reynolds' father had been a leading member.

Then Hunt, crippled in an attack by a marauding bear, sold out to Parkhurst who came representing overseas British interests. That was the birth of the Trans Continental Ranch.

The valley comprised a lush ninety-mile length, in places fifty miles wide. The headquarters Luther Hunt had chosen, which still remained the main TC ranch, stood on a high bank above the river, twenty miles south of Kernville, the county seat and the only real town in the great valley.

Below this main ranch, between the escarpment of high mountains, lifted a ten-mile-wide saddle, a broad pass letting into Middle Park and on to the railroad. On the north the mountains closed together and rose in ranks of sweeping rock badlands, those same trackless, inhospitable barriers through which Boyd Reynolds had ridden to make his re-entry into the valley.

There was no trail through these broken, rock-studded reaches which cattle could navigate. The only real exit was the southern pass which TC sat astride like a guardian dragon at the mouth of a cave.

So long as Luther Hunt had controlled the valley there had been a single, common roundup each year, a single trail herd flowing south toward the shipping point on the railroad. There, the animals were tallied before being loaded into the cars, and each individual rancher then received his payment from the cattle buyer.

But even before Boyd Reynolds had left the valley this habit had changed. The weight of the absentee ownership of the big ranch rested heavily on the smaller ranchers, who were forced to drive their herds in a sweeping arc, along the lower slopes of the hills, to avoid the TC drift fences, picking their own uncertain way to the rails.

The Running R was the northernmost ranch of the smaller outfits. Its home buildings were sturdily constructed of logs, built like a fort to repel the earlier Indian raids, and it sat beside the clear, rushing stream only two miles below where the waters escaped the canyon and entered the valley floor.

22

Boyd Reynolds reached it just before daybreak. He rode alone, leaving his newly recruited crew raking through the ruins of the Crossing, trying to assemble what few things of value had survived the holocaust.

He circled warily, fully conscious that his birthplace was now held as TC's northern line camp, noting with a dull anger the neglect that now disgraced the place.

His mother's kitchen garden, once a thing of beauty, tidy and accented with small, surprise clumps of blooming flowers along the river's brim, lay weed-grown, unused, trampled.

The roof of the blacksmith shop had blown partly away and remained unrepaired. There were a dozen horses in the pole corral, and smoke lifted lazily from the cookshack's chimney, but there was no further sign of life.

He completed his wide circle and returned to the main trail, running taut as a tightened string down the center of the valley to Kernville, forty miles away.

He did not hurry, but the steady lope of his broad-chested horse ate through the miles. Occasionally he stopped, granting short rests to his trail-gaunted animal, and three times he made side swings to look more closely at knots of cattle which grazed along the stream's meandering course.

The first group held nearly fifty animals. They were spooky, raising their heads to examine him with uncertainty as he approached, but his heart leaped, for even at the distance he could make out the familiar brand, the Running R.

Apparently Jud Laws was boldly using the brands he had purchased, for some private reason of his own.

Boyd swung back to the trail and drove forward, but it was midafternoon before he made out the irregular line that Kernville's buildings thrust into the mountain air.

He knew he was still a good five miles short of the town. Distance was deceptive at this altitude. But at length he entered the head of the long main street. He crossed Moccasin Creek, which cut out of the western hills to add its crystal waters to the Hunt, then climbed the gentle rise on which the town was built.

It was a drab community, a cow town, nothing more. It drew its small sustenance from the surrounding ranchers and their scattered employees, owing its existence solely to their needs and to the fact that the cut-stone courthouse represented the center of the only law within forty-five hundred square miles.

For the most part, the buildings were board and batten, and few of the walls had ever known paint. The wide planks had weathered under the fierce summer sun and grayed with the wind-driven winter blizzards until they looked more like pewter than wood.

Bisecting the main roadway were three cross streets which ran out to lose themselves in the surrounding grasslands. Beyond the four-block business center, circling it with a protective rim, were the loosely grouped houses of the town's inhabitants, built each according to its owner's whim, without regard to its position in relation to its neighbors.

The bank, the two-story hotel, and three saloons dominated the central intersection. The courthouse stood in a grass plot a block square, facing the main road, its jail entrance on the side street. The sheriff's home sat beyond the jail, a plank house, contrasting sharply with the solid stone building. Behind the courthouse were spaced a general store, a blacksmith shop and a corral.

Boyd rode the length of the street, noting that only half a dozen people were abroad in the heat of the late afternoon sun. He turned his horse into the open runway of the livery barn beside the corral.

The hostler was old, bent by time and rheumatism until he walked crablike, his upper body slanted forward so that it seemed impossible that he could keep his balance. He came forward as Boyd stepped down and stared at him uncertainly, his nutcracker jaws under a two-day beard working nervously.

"Ain't you Boyd Reynolds? Naw . . . you can't be. He's dead."

"I'm Boyd, Horace, and I'm not dead. Rub him down and give him some grain. He hasn't had any in a week."

He turned to the saddle, loosening it, swinging it down to drape it across the rack beside the open doorway of the barn office. Then, shouldering his saddlebags, he caught up his rifle and moved into the street.

He passed the courthouse and reached the main cross-roads. The hotel occupied one corner. The bank was diagonally across from it. The other two corners held saloons.

After the chill of the high hills he was feeling the low country heat. Dust from the road stirred as a wagon moved past him, a woman and two children perched on its seat. The woman glanced at him with full curiosity, her face looking unnaturally old from constant exposure to the harsh weather, her dress a washed-out print, faded past recognition of its original pattern.

Two small girls ran boisterously from Landers' store beyond the hotel, their mouths full, their small cheeks sticky with candy, separating to pass him, giggling at some precious secret of their own. Two riders rode by from the south without glancing in his direction, and Old Tate, the swamper of the Paradise Saloon, shuffled through the batwing doors to dump his scrub bucket into the gutter dust.

Boyd had the unreal sensation that he had never been away, that four years had brought no change to this sleepy town. But he knew that there had been change, no matter what the surface appearances were. He reached the hotel and tramped into it.

The low-ceilinged lobby was stifling and dark after the brightness of the sun-filled street, and it took his eyes a minute to readjust to see that the row of caned chairs against the right wall was empty, that there was no one behind the tall desk at the foot of the uncarpeted stairs.

A bell tinkled as he let the street door swing shut, propelled by its spring hinges, and Dan Hay appeared from the inner office. He was a big man with a round dome of a head completely bald of hair. His nose was too small for the expanse of his face, and his eyes were shrouded under heavy brows as if they tried to make up the lack of hair on his scalp.

Boyd Reynolds had never known him well. It was seldom that he and his friends had used the hotel, preferring to roll in their blankets in the hay of the livery barn when they stayed in town. But in a place as small as Kernville everyone knew everyone else at least to nod to, and he watched the slow recognition and surprise open up Hay's face.

"Boyd Reynolds?"

"That's right."

"Heard you were dead."

"A mistake."

The hotel man scrubbed his chin with a pale hand. "Well, sir. I never expected to see you again. You'll find a few changes around the country." His eyes fixed on Reynolds' face. "Some you won't like."

"That's what I've heard."

Hay hesitated as if he wanted to say more, then changed his mind. "You want a room?"

Reynolds nodded. The man turned, lifted down a key, and hesitated again. Then with a shrug which seemed to indicate that it was none of his business, he passed the key across the scarred desk.

Boyd climbed the stairs. He moved along the creaking boards of the narrow upper hall to the far end and pushed open the door of number twelve.

The room was like a thousand other rooms in the small cow-town hotels. Its plank walls had been covered with flour sacking over which a flowered paper had been pasted. In places the paper was torn, exposing the cloth and sometimes the boards beneath.

The bed was narrow, its springs sagging in the middle beneath the pitifully thin mattress of husks, the white-enamel frame chipped to show the rusting iron where a hundred riders had rested their spurred heels.

A wooden wardrobe, a washstand with flowered bowl and pitcher, a single straight chair, completed the meager furnishings.

The bed was unmade, its mattress ticking worn, faded and stained.

Noise at the door made Boyd swing around. The knock was repeated and he shifted his gun belt a little so that the heavy revolver rode straight against the flatness of his thigh.

"Come in."

The door was pushed inward and he saw a brown-haired girl, her arms loaded with a blanket, sheets and towel. She entered wordlessly, laying her burden on the foot of the bed.

26

Then she turned to face him and a smile twisted the wideness of her full-lipped mouth.

"Hi, Boyd. You don't remember me, do you?"

He was looking back through the card index of memory. Her face had a ghost of familiarity. It was a slightly chubby face, still holding the remnant softness of immaturity. Her eyes were brown, large, her nose a trifle short, but her mouth was generous and the smile very friendly.

Association made him say, "You must be Jenny Hay."

"You do remember." She sounded pleased. "I don't know how. I was just a kid when I saw you last."

He judged that she could not be over seventeen now, eighteen at the outside. He tried to recall something about her, some shared memory or experience, and failed. They had gone to the same school, but since he was six or seven years her senior, they had never known each other, and he had stopped school at seventeen. At that time she would have been perhaps twelve.

"I didn't expect you to remember," she said. "I used to see you at the dances. You even danced with me once. It was at the Flint Ridge schoolhouse."

He recalled it vaguely. In his last year there they had held what they called a mixed-age dance. Each of the older boys had been asked to dance one square with a younger girl.

"Sure," he said. "I know."

Her smile widened to a gamin grin. "I'm mighty glad you're alive, Boyd. I was sure surprised when Paw told me you were here. He's real worried about it. You shouldn't have come back, you know." Pain rose behind her soft eyes. "You'd better take out while you can. The country's not the same."

He said, "That's what everybody tells me, but I've got things to do."

"Don't do them." She sounded very anxious, putting out one hand as if to stop him. "Don't get yourself hurt. I couldn't stand that."

He gave her a quick smile, then went out and down the hall, wondering why whatever happened to him should be of concern to her.

The interior of the bank had not changed. It was a long room flanked by two writing desks on one side, a counter on the other. At the rear was the office of the cashier.

It was after hours when Boyd Reynolds knocked on the front door, but banking hours had never been rigid in Kernville. He could recall a time the institution had been opened one midnight to accommodate his father.

His knock was answered by Mark Austin. Mark had been teller for as long as Boyd could remember. He was a dried-up little gnome with a long, curling mustache of which he was very proud, and he looked at Boyd with growing astonishment.

"Where'd you come from? You're dead."

Boyd was getting tired of being told this. He nodded briefly. "Is Petrie in?" His voice was abrupt.

"In his office," said Mark, and stepped back to let him pass, a hurt showing in his mild face.

During Boyd's childhood Leonard Petrie had been an impressive figure. He had a shock of heavy black hair, beginning to gray at the temples, and a booming voice that would have done credit to a senator. He had always dressed in a long-tailed broadcloth coat and striped trousers, entirely out of keeping with the rest of Kernville. He lived in a white square house at the head of Cottonwood Avenue, and his wife had been the social arbiter of the town.

In some ways Boyd had felt closer to the banker than to his own father, and from the time of his first memory he had thought of the Petrie house as a second home. It was to Petrie he had talked when he decided to go away, and he felt certain now that if he could count on help from anyone in the valley, it would come from Petrie.

He pushed open the door of the corner office and stepped into the room. Leonard Petrie was at his desk, and Boyd experienced an immediate shock at his appearance. The man had aged enormously in the four years. His face, which had been full and cherubic, looked as sunken as if all his teeth had been removed, and he sat hunched, his big shoulders seeming to bear far too heavy a load.

He looked up inquiringly, annoyance pinching at his dark

eyes. Then they changed and his mouth slacked off in surprise.

"Boyd Reynolds."

Boyd shut the door. He crossed the room and extended his hand above the desk. "How are you, Uncle Leonard?"

The banker put his pen down slowly. He made no effort to take the hand. It was as though he were afraid of touching a ghost.

"Boyd Reynolds . . ." he said again.

Some of the annoyance Boyd had been building against the story of his death rode up into his voice.

"I'm alive." He said shortly. "Apparently the San Francisco police found the body of a man who robbed me."

The banker leaned back slowly, his chair creaking in protest.

"Alive . . . yes . . . alive . . ." He ran the tip of his tongue around his sallow lips. Then he seemed to realize how discourteous he sounded, and waved a hand. "Sit down, boy. Give an old man a chance to get used to a new idea." He smiled faintly at his words, but there was no humor in the gesture.

"So . . . you're back. I suppose you've heard about your brother?"

"I've heard."

"We never found out what happened. And the ranch?"

"I've heard that, too." Boyd took the facing chair, sitting on its edge, leaning forward to rest his hand on the edge of the desk. "That's one of the things I want to see you about. But first, how are Mrs. Petrie and Ellen?"

"Why . . . why, they're fine . . ." There was something in Petrie's manner that Boyd did not understand, a certain evasiveness which had not been there in the old days.

"Ellen at home?"

The man nodded uncertainly.

"I'll go up and see her in a little while. First though, I've got to begin getting the ranch back."

"Back?" The banker straightened with shock. "But, Boyd, don't you comprehend? The ranch is gone. It was sold at a sheriff's sale to T.C. I'm afraid it will be impossible for you to get it back. Even if you have the money."

"I haven't," Boyd said, "Not enough to buy it. But I don't believe I have to buy what is already mine." His voice was sharper than he'd intended it to be. "When I left here, there was no mortgage against the Running R. I don't see how it could legally be mortgaged without my agreement. I am half owner."

Petrie started to speak quickly, checked himself and said in a measured tone, "Your brother applied for the mortgage. We had the word of the San Francisco police that you were dead. The bank lent the money to Hugh."

"But I am not dead."

Petrie stared, opening and closing his mouth, and Boyd saw the helplessness in the old man's face. He knew a moment of sympathy for him. This was, he reasoned, not Petrie's fault. The banker had apparently made the loan in good faith.

Then he remembered the attack by the TC the night before, recalled the intimation that Jud Laws had had his brother murdered, and his resolve hardened. If he was going to fight, he must fight all the way, no matter who got hurt in the process.

"I don't know what to say . . ." Petrie finally managed, spreading his hands in a vague gesture. "I don't . . . I know how you feel . . . but my first duty is to the bank. I—I'll have to have legal advice . . ."

"I guess I will, too." Boyd Reynolds stood up. He saw no point in continuing this conversation at the moment.

Behind him Petrie cleared his throat. "Boyd, I don't suppose you'd take advice from me?"

Boyd stopped. He turned slowly, feeling a fresh hurt at his old mentor's loss of stature. "I always have."

"Let the ranch go. You can't win. There isn't a lawyer in the country who would take your case, no matter what fee you might offer. There's too much power against you, too much ruthless force. I don't want the thing that happened to Hugh to happen to you. If I'd realized—"

He stopped, as if regretting what he had already said, then added in a different tone, "Listen, son. I'm not as well off as I used to be. In fact, I never had as much as many in this valley think. But I'll be glad to help you get some kind of a start, somewhere else."

Boyd was watching him closely. He said suddenly, "What are you afraid of, Leonard?"

The old man lifted his head. "Afraid? I'm afraid for you."

"Because of Jud Laws?"

The man behind the desk flinched a little, but he said steadily, "Because of Jud Laws. Jud is ruthless, and he's grown pretty big since you went away. He's the most important man in the valley. He's as important as anyone in the state."

"He hasn't changed." There was contempt in Reynolds' tone. "He always was a sneaking, grasping little man. I could lick him then and I can beat him now."

He did not wait for an answer. He swung about and went out, past the gaping Austin, without glancing in the old teller's direction. Not until he reached the street did he pause in his rapid, anger-ridden stride. Then he stopped, forcing himself to relax. He lit a cigar and looked up and down the thoroughfare, wondering what he could do.

His eye caught a sign in the window above the Landers store: *Bolger Roberts, Attorney at Law.*

His eye held on the sign, considering.

Bolger Roberts had been a top man in the valley once, but even before Boyd had left, the lawyer had been known as the town drunk. What few cases came to him he fumbled away, spending the better part of his time sitting morosely at a rear table in the Paradise saloon or sleeping on the ancient sofa in his office.

Reynolds had no doubt that Petrie was right in saying no lawyer in the county would dare to stand against Jud Laws, for if the man's hold on local politics was as tight as it seemed, they would be signing their professional death warrant in taking the case against him.

But Old Man Roberts had nothing much to lose. He had no practice to speak of. It just might be.

Boyd started deliberately toward the stairway which led up beside the store building, hesitated, changed his mind and angled across to the Paradise.

Inside, four riders were lined against the counter, talking

aimlessly. They fell silent as he stepped in and turned to study him curiously. He paid them no attention, pausing at the front end of the bar, his eyes seeking the rear table and not finding Roberts in the room. The bartender came forward. Boyd bought a pint bottle of whiskey, stuck it in his pocket and left the saloon.

He angled back across the street and climbed the stairs, the old boards bending dangerously under his solid weight. The office door hung open a few inches and he shoved it inward without bothering to knock.

The dusty room beyond held a roll-top desk, two shelves on which reposed the battered books of a law library, a table with a letter press, two chairs and the sofa. On the sofa, fully dressed even to his crumpled fedora hat, Bolger Roberts slept. He slept on his back, snoring gently, his wispy white beard rising and falling with every inhalation of his narrow chest.

Boyd Reynolds stood and watched him. This was one man who had not altered in the past four years. He had looked like death then. He looked like death now.

Reynolds went on to the rear room. Here was a narrow, bunklike bed, an iron sink with a pitcher pump whose pipe ran down to the well behind the store, a battered stove and a tin-topped table. He found coffee in the blackened pot, started a fire in the stove and, removing an iron lid, set the pot above the flames. Not until the coffee boiled did he disturb the sleeper.

He poured a steaming cup, carried it back to the office, and shook the lawyer awake.

Bolger Roberts opened bloodshot eyes, pink as those of a white rabbit. He lay staring upward reproachfully at his tormentor for a full minute as reason slowly returned, then he closed his eyes tightly, muttering.

"I know I'm dead. I know I'll never see Boyd Reynolds again this side of Hell."

Reynolds said, "You're not seeing things, Borg. It's Boyd, and we're both alive."

The lawyer's eyes opened again. He sat up unsteadily. He saw the steaming coffee cup and winced. Then Boyd took the pint bottle from his pocket and laced the dark liquid heavily. The old eyes glistened. The clawlike hands came out to clutch the cup and he raised it to his blue shrunken lips.

The coffee was so hot, he shuddered, but he drank it down, then held out the cup.

"Just one straight shot." His tone was a pleading whine.

"Later," Boyd said, thrusting the cork into the bottle and dropping it back into his pocket. "I want you sober enough to talk business."

"Business? Now I know you're dead—at least your mind is. You know I haven't really tried a case in ten years."

Reynolds said bluntly, "I haven't any choice, Borg. I'm going to take back the Running R, and Petrie says there isn't a lawyer in the county who will buck Jud Laws."

The old man grinned mischievously. "He's right. There's not a man around will stand against Laws, not even Petrie."

"Why should Petrie be afraid of him?"

"Gimme a drink."

Reynolds hesitated, then produced the bottle. The lawyer uncorked it with trembling, white fingers. He took a long swallow from the neck, recorked it carefully, and handed it back to Reynolds.

"Because Laws owns the bank—just as he owns about everything else in the valley."

Reynolds showed his surprise. "Petrie's bank? How did he manage that?"

"Like he manages everything. He got Petrie into a personal cattle deal, then held off shipping until the market broke. Petrie had to sell bank stock to cover his loans. When the smoke cleared he found it was Laws who'd bought his stock."

Reynolds could think of nothing to say.

The lawyer chuckled. "But there's more than one way to skin a cat. Petrie's girl has her cap set for Laws. Looks like the old man will get back by marriage more than he lost on the cattle deal."

Reynolds felt a dropping sickness at the words. A picture of Ellen rose before his eyes. She was, he knew, the prettiest girl he had ever seen, with her blue eyes that looked like

33

corn flowers, her taffy hair, her pert little nose and up-tilted chin.

Ellen Petrie and Jud Laws. It wasn't possible. And sitting there he realized something that he had not thought of before: he wanted Ellen Petrie more than he wanted the Running R.

The lawyer looked at him with eyes which were beginning to clear and now held an animal sharpness.

"Always figured you had some interest in that direction yourself. Used to see you kids at dances. Made a good-looking couple, you did."

Reynolds could not bring himself to talk about it. He said instead, "I'm going to take back the ranch."

Bolger Roberts arched an eyebrow. "You are, now? And just how do you figure to work that one?"

Boyd said, "I was half owner. I did not agree to that mortgage. I did not sign it. I had no say when my property was sold out from under me."

Roberts considered. "You may have a point there—but if you were half owner, so was your brother. If the mortgage was no good, then he got an unsecured loan from the bank. They'll levee on his estate, which would be half of the ranch and stock you recover, plus interest. They'll tie you up in court for years."

"That's your side of it. You file the necessary papers tomorrow. I'll take back the ranch and cattle. Find out how many cows were included in that sale."

The old man snorted. "You haven't a chance. There's not one local judge would find for you."

"What about the state courts?"

"You got the money to carry it up there?"

"I'll get it."

"And you still maybe won't get a hearing. Jud Laws' influence goes pretty high."

"You're afraid of him, too?"

The old man laughed. It had been a long time since anyone had heard him laugh.

"Son," he said, "when you get as old as I am, and as full of whiskey as I am, the only thing you fear is that the distilleries will go out of business before you drink yourself to death. I'm not afraid of anything. I'll take your case. Just give me enough to stay half drunk. I can't think straight sober any more."

For answer Boyd pulled out the half-empty bottle and shoved it into the old man's hand.

"If it helps," he said, "I know Governor Pratt. Wyatt Earp introduced me to him in Denver."

CHAPTER FOUR

BOYD REYNOLDS walked the length of the side street, meeting no one he knew. The Petrie house stood on a small rise, the yard around it a well-kept grass lawn enclosed within a neat picket fence.

The sun had dropped behind the valley's western rim, but the smell of heat and dust still choked the early evening air. Boyd unlatched and opened the gate, followed the boardwalk and climbed the two steps to the deep porch. Within him was a turbulence of conflicting emotions. Ellen and the Running R. Ellen and Jud Laws. Ellen's and his memories; memories that had sustained him through the long period of homesickness, that had haunted him and finally brought him home. Lovely Ellen, so close now, just beyond the door. He stopped, nearly turning back, caught in a quick rush of mute fear like a boy on his first visit to a girl.

Vines climbed the porch posts at either end, cloistering the area in blue shadows. He stood, his breathing uneven, looking back across the straggling town. Then with a swift decision he knocked on the door.

It opened almost at once, as if she had been standing behind it in the box hall, awaiting his arrival.

"Boyd Reynolds. Father told us you were alive, that you had been to the bank."

She was older. She had lost the stringy schoolgirl look, but her eyes were the same and the taffy hair differed only in that it was now softly coiled around her small head

35

instead of hanging in the two thick braids down her back. "It's good to see you."

Without quite being conscious of what he did he reached forward, grasping both of her small hands. For an instant she tried to pull away, then she relaxed, leaving them in his hold, yet not returning his pressure.

His smile was tight and difficult. "Don't I get a kiss?"

She stiffened. "Boyd, please—"

His voice came tight, unnatural in his own ears. "You kissed me when I went away. You said you'd wait."

She looked at him in blank astonishment. "Wait? You never wrote. For nearly three years I've thought you dead. What was I to wait for?"

Guilt rode sharply through him. How could he tell her that a stubborn pride had kept him from writing?

"I told you I'd come for you when I had something to offer that wasn't half Hugh's. I'm sorry you thought I was dead. I'm more than sorry that I heard you are going with Jud Laws. Surely you wouldn't marry him?"

Her chin went up and she pulled her fingers from him. "It's no secret. And you've no right to say anything. I'm twenty-three years old, and quite capable of choosing my husband myself."

A blinding confusion engulfed him. He had ridden over a thousand miles to come home, urged on by an urgent need to be with his own people. The restlessness which had sent him forth, which had been a part of growing up, was gone. Now he had come home, only to find his brother murdered, his ranch stolen, his girl turning to the man responsible.

He could not blame her for not waiting, since she believed him dead. She had been motivated by the need to live, to plan her life differently. Yet it was all wrong that she should choose Jud Laws, so miserably unworthy of her love. He blamed her for this. It hurt deeply. In a twisted way it reflected on the quality of his long-held feeling for her. To see the one he had always considered above reproach degrade herself thus was like a physical pain, an ache that went through him and drained his strength.

And like a child he struck out at her. "So I turn my back and you throw yourself at the lowest animal in sight."

36

Her eyes changed, deepening with quick fury until they were almost black. Her hand half rose to slap him, then she checked herself, stepping back, saying in a chill voice:

"You'd better go, Boyd."

At once he was contrite. "Ellen." His voice shook against all his control. "I'm sorry. I didn't mean that. You know I didn't. You've got me confused. Please. I'm back. Give me time. Just a little time. I can make you happy. He'll only cause you sorrow. Ellen—"

She stood unbending, unforgiving. "I think not. The past is past, Boyd. Get on your horse and ride out of Hunt Valley. Your friends are gone, your ranch is gone. There is nothing here you need, and no one here who needs you. Most assuredly not I."

Instead of helping, she was twisting the hurt deeper. Through the jumble of his thoughts he knew it was deliberate, and by sheer will he forced his passions down.

"I see," he said at last. "You'd like me to ride out, to leave you and Jud to own the world. I'm sorry. I'm not going to throw in the hand. I'm back and I mean to have what belongs to me. Tell Jud that. Tell him I'm back to stay. He may have whipped everyone else in the valley, but I'm here and I'm not going to be whipped."

He turned on his heel then, without waiting for any answer, and strode rapidly down the walk. He had almost reached the gate when he heard the horse and looked up. Jud Laws was coming toward him down the street at a half trot.

Boyd pulled the gate open and stepped through, waiting until the mounted man reached his side and dropped spiderlike to the ground. He had been waiting for this meeting with the TC manager, but he had not wanted it here, not with Ellen watching from the porch.

Jud Laws was still several inches shorter than Reynolds, but his body had thickened, and now he looked almost square. His hair was black. His face had an Indian cast, the cheekbones high, the mouth thin with a cruel twist. He looked Reynolds up and down, contempt, which he made no effort to conceal, in his manner.

"I heard you were around here again."

37

Reynolds said, "Bad news usually travels fast, Jud."

"Bad news for whom?" Laws laughed, no music in the sound. "If you think your return worries me, think again, Reynolds. There's nothing you can do, nothing but get yourself killed if you're foolish."

"The way my brother did?"

Laws' shrug was careless. "If you like it that way, yes."

He pushed past Boyd and went up the walk with the certain tread of a man who knows that he has his world in his pocket. Reynolds watched him go, more furious than he had ever been in his life, stilling an impulse to pull the heavy gun at his hip and send a bullet crashing into Laws' broad back.

He saw the shorter man mount the steps, grasp the slender hands that he had so recently held, draw the girl into his burly arms and kiss her thoroughly.

It was as if they savored the knowledge that he witnessed their embrace, as if both tried purposely to hurt him further. He turned and moved blindly up the street.

Inside him, emotions struggled in a battle which shook him as nothing else ever had. Bitterness all but rode him under.

He reached the intersection, stood stricken with sudden aimlessness, then walked in perverse determination toward the Paradise Saloon.

It was the supper hour and he half expected to find the long room deserted. There were, however, half a dozen men against the bar, and with a start he recognized Max Cleaver in their midst. The TC foreman looked even bigger than he had on the preceding night in Alf Bentley's bar.

For the barest instant Reynolds hesitated, caution whispering its warning in his head. But he was beyond clear reason now. He wanted nothing more than to fight the world. And if the fight came this night, he would welcome it, no matter what the odds.

He moved to the bar, a dozen feet from the bunched riders, and motioned for the single bartender to bring him a bottle and glass. He poured a full drink and almost threw it down his throat.

The bartender eyed him narrowly and said in a low voice,

"You don't remember me. I'm Joe Connors. I was just a kid when you went away."

Boyd poured himself another drink without appearing to hear. Connors' voice dropped another notch.

"Those guys at the other end are laying for you. Laws' orders. He came in with them ten minutes ago. A guy who spotted you when you bought that pint told him you were back."

Reynolds glanced at him. "Thanks."

Connors shrugged. "You'd better leave."

"Thanks again."

Irritation crept in Connors' tone. "Don't thank me. I just don't want this place wrecked."

Boyd Reynolds had a sudden, wild desire to laugh. No one in the whole stinking town cared what happened to him. Even this silly bartender was only worrying about his fixtures. His voice was petulantly surly.

"This is a public place."

The man gaped at him.

"I drink where I please." He poured a third shot. The liquor ran down his throat like fingers of fire.

He was conscious that the TC men were shifting down toward him, that Connors abruptly found occupation elsewhere. He glanced up, watching them in the mirror above the back-bar.

Max Cleaver put down his glass. He said something to his men in an undertone, then moved toward Reynolds, coming against the bar at his elbow. He reached out deliberately, took Reynolds' partly filled bottle, raised it, filling his mouth with liquor. He set the bottle back in place, then, still with deliberation, spat the whiskey directly into Boyd's face.

Boyd hit him. The action was triggered by instinct. He was half blinded by the alcohol that had struck the bridge of his nose and spattered into his eyes.

His fist crashed into the bigger man's mouth, crushing the lips and cutting Boyd's knuckles on the prominent teeth.

Max Cleaver took two steps backward to avoid falling. He steadied himself by catching at the edge of the bar, and spat out a tooth through his bloody lips.

Then he charged.

Boyd swept the whiskey bottle from the bar, bringing it up, then down on the man's head. Cleaver's upthrust hand broke part of the force of the blow, but he staggered nonetheless. The bottle had fractured in Boyd's hand, leaving him holding only the neck.

It was too short to serve as a weapon and he dropped it as Cleaver's huge arms closed about him. The man was groggy, but he clung there, dumping his full weight against Reynolds.

Boyd writhed, trying to break the encircling grip, but Cleaver was too strong. He had his fingers locked together, and gradually he bent Boyd backward until he threatened to crush his victim's spine.

Boyd jackknifed his knees, falling purposely, bringing his attacker down on top of him. The weight drove the air from his lungs, and both lay thus for a full second, too spent by the quick fury of the action to make any effort. Then Boyd got a heel against the bar and kicked away, rolling them toward the center of the room.

Somewhere in the roll Boyd managed to break Cleaver's grip. He came swiftly to his knees as the other tried to rise, his senses reeling. Then someone hit him from behind.

He went flat on his face. Three men jumped on him. He tried to fight back, all of his pent-up frustration lending him strength, but he had no chance.

His senses swayed. He knew that he was taking a thorough beating. A heavy boot cracked against his jaw, another kick nearly collapsed his ribs.

And then they weren't there any more.

He lay gasping, trying for breath, fighting to clear his clouding mind, appalled at the stupidity which had led him into the brutal and senseless fight. He saw a pair of boots come toward him and thought that the attack was being renewed, and fully expected to be kicked to death.

Instead, he heard a voice growl above him. "Come on. Get up."

He was still on his face. Somehow he got his hands under his chest, although the arms felt devoid of strength, and with much effort rocked up to his hands and knees. He

40

stayed there, trying to recover enough breath to move further, then crawled blindly to the bar, reaching its corner, using it as a kind of ladder to help drag himself upward to his feet.

He stood splay-footed, rocking back and forth, his palms pressed against the scarred surface, his body sagging forward. And suddenly he was sick.

He vomited, the whiskey he had drunk coming first, the acid burning the cuts inside his mouth. His body shuddered under the effort, and it was minutes before the retching passed.

Slowly he turned his head. The room wheeled. He saw Max Cleaver at the far end of the bar. The big foreman was being supported by his fellows. He seemed in no better shape than Boyd himself.

Then he saw Sheriff Dodsworth and realized who had stopped the carnage. Tom Dodsworth was built like a tree trunk. He was a good twenty years older than Reynolds, and had been first deputy, then sheriff for as long as Boyd could remember.

He had two men with him, both wearing deputy badges. The deputies stood beside the door, their guns in their hands but not pointing at anyone. Dodsworth came forward to where Boyd still clung to the bar.

"You all right?" His voice held only professional concern.

Boyd wiped his mouth on the sleeve of his shirt. He stared at the blood mixed with vomit on the bar and wondered if something inside him was ruptured or if the red came from his external cuts.

His mouth tasted foul. He twisted and, seeing the bartender, said, "Whiskey." The word was little more than a croak.

The man did not move. Dodsworth said, "Give him a drink."

Connors brought a bottle and glass, handing them to Boyd. Reynolds dropped the glass on the floor and drank directly from the bottle. The liquor seered his lacerated mouth, but it took away the ugly taste.

He shook his head slowly then, still holding the bottle. "I guess I'm all right."

41

"Okay. Come on then."

"Where to?"

"I'm locking you up."

"For what?"

Dodsworth's voice was expressionless. "For coming in here and starting a fight."

Reynolds wiped his mouth again. "I didn't start it."

"They say you did." He jerked his head toward the group.

Reynolds looked along the bar at the TC men, and found them grinning at his discomfiture. Even Cleaver managed a weak smile through his broken lips.

Reynolds glanced toward the bartender. The man was busy cleaning up the mess and refused to meet his eye. Boyd knew he would get no help from that direction.

He shrugged. There was no use in arguing with Dodsworth. He took a step away from the bar, swayed and would have fallen had not Dodsworth caught his arm. The sheriff steadied him with one hand; with the other he reached across and took Reynolds' gun, which by some miracle had remained in the holster. Then he marched out through the door with the deputies closing in to follow. Behind him Reynolds heard the TC laughter, and at the moment did not care.

The jail had been built with the courthouse, some ten years before. It smelled of dust, old forgotten prisoners, and antiseptic. They herded him into the office, across that, and placed him in one of the two cells. As the door closed and the lock ground over, Reynolds turned to look squarely at the sheriff.

"How long you going to keep me here?" His voice sounded muddy.

"Until the court meets next week."

"Why? You never hold a prisoner more than overnight for a fight."

Dodsworth's craggy face was expressionless. "I'm holding you longer."

"Why? Because Jud Laws told you to?"

Dodsworth did not answer.

42

"At least let me talk to Bolger Roberts. A man has the right to talk to his lawyer."

"Maybe. In the morning."

"Now, listen—"

"You listen," Dodsworth told him in a flat voice. "If I hadn't showed up when I did that bunch would have killed you. I'm keeping you locked up until you get some sense and agree to get on a horse and clear out of this county. The word is out to get you. I've been told there's a five-hundred-dollar price tag on your hide. And there are plenty of guns riding for the TC who would think nothing of knocking off a man for one hundred."

Reynolds looked at him, saying nothing.

"You're a damn fool," Dodsworth went on. His voice still showed no emotion. He was as dispassionate as death. "You can't beat Jud Laws. No one can, and those of us who stayed here know it."

He turned and walked away, leaving Reynolds with his thoughts. They were in nowise pleasant, and hope seemed dim indeed.

CHAPTER FIVE

SUNLIGHT sent its path across the dirty floor of the small cell, seeping in between the three bars which guarded the single window.

Boyd Reynolds lay on his back for several moments after he roused. He did not know what had waked him. No sound came from the jail office beyond the grilled door; no sound came through the jail window from the rear street.

He lay not moving, every muscle and cord in his big body a dull, aching thing. His lips were cut and puffed, and the terrible acrid taste was back in his mouth.

Finally he twisted, putting his booted feet on the floor

and sitting up slowly, feeling his head spin, feeling the burning sensation behind his eyes.

He rose, using his arms to push up from the thin pad that served as a mattress, since he did not trust his knees to lift him. He stood swaying, trying to get his balance, like a drunk who had been deprived of alcohol too long.

There was a wooden washstand on the far side of the cell, a tin pan on its scarred top, a bucket of water and a slop pail on the floor beside it.

He crossed. He sloshed cold water into the pan and used his stiff hands like scoops to splash the water against his puffy face. He was fully dressed, for he had been too beaten to care, and neither the sheriff nor the deputies had even offered to give him a hand toward undressing.

The water dribbled from his face, down across the shirt, to mingle with the crusted blood which had dried there. He took no notice. He picked up the bucket and deliberately poured it over his aching head. Then he sat down on the bunk, breathing deeply.

A noise in the outer office brought him to the grilled door. "What about a smoke?"

The deputy sitting at the desk turned his head. "So you came out of it." He had a lean face with a tight mouth and cold, gray eyes. A scar started at the corner of his left lid, pulling it down in what looked like a half wink, then ran on across his cheek, a bit of ugly tissue, angry red.

"What about a smoke? I had tobacco when I came in here."

The man hesitated. He was not fundamentally cruel, but life had left him with little real feeling. He pulled out a desk drawer, found the partly filled cloth sack, papers, and brought a handful of matches.

"If you get gay and try to fire the joint, I'll gut-shoot you."

Boyd did not bother to answer. He received the tobacco between the bars, carried it back to the bunk and sat down. His fingers trembled as he built the smoke, but once it was between his lips it steadied him. He sat quietly, smoking one cigarette after another. Finally he lifted his head, hearing a new voice in the office.

Then Jenny Hay was before the barred door, the deputy behind her. She carried a tray wth two covered dishes, a cup and coffeepot, and a bundle under her arm.

"I brought you some food and some clean clothes, and a razor. I got them from your bed roll."

He started to get up. The deputy said, "Stay where you are, cowboy." He found his keys and opened the door, motioning the girl to put the tray on the stand.

She obeyed, putting the bundle carefully beside it, then without looking at Boyd she turned and went back through the door, followed by the deputy.

Boyd called, "Thanks."

She did not answer. He heard her steps recede across the office and heard the outer door close. The deputy locked the door behind him and moved away. Not until then did Reynolds rise.

There were two eggs and some bacon on one plate, a pile of toasted bread on the other. The thought of food made his stomach turn over, but he forced himself to eat. The coffeepot held four cups, and he drank them all, slowly, feeling the warmth relax his knotted stomach muscles.

Basically he was in good physical shape. Hard work and hard riding had kept excess weight off him. He felt better as he smoked two more cigarettes. Then he rose and shaved.

There was no mirror, and he had to feel for his whiskers, using the strong lye soap which had been on the stand beside the basin. It stung his cuts, but he ignored this. Afterwards he used the last of the water to sponge off his body, found a clean shirt and clean socks in the bundle, and put them on.

When he returned to his seat on the bunk, he felt like a different person. He was still battered and sore, but his native vitality had taken over.

He sat for perhaps an hour before the next interruption. Again the outer door opened, and he heard Bolger Roberts' voice. He realized at once that the old man was drunk, and quick anger rode up in him.

Every way he turned he seemed to be blocked. Even his lawyer could not stay sober long enough to help him. He did not bother to get up as the deputy came to the door.

45

Roberts swayed in. He was unshaven, his eyes bloodshot, and his clothes looked slept in. He waited until the deputy locked him inside with his client, then he said in an accusing tone:

"You kind of raised hell."

Boyd Reynolds swore. "Did you stagger down here just to tell me that?"

"I came to give you advice." The old man's words were slurred, but Boyd saw that he was not as drunk as he appeared.

"Don't bother."

"That's what a lawyer is for, to bother. If more people asked legal advice before they jumped into things, there wouldn't be so much trouble in the world."

"You don't seem to have done so well."

Roberts came forward to stand above his client. "Do as I say, son, not as I do. Now, I've been talking to our honorable sheriff. I have known him for a long time. I knew him, in fact, before power corrupted and warped him; when he had the shreds of honor to wrap about him."

"Stop it. Go back to your office and sleep it off."

Roberts paid no attention. "The sheriff agrees with me. He can see no reason for your untimely death. If you would simply listen to reason—"

Reynolds stood up. By doing so he towered above the older man. His voice was too low to carry to the jail office, but each word was flat and hard and final.

"Bolger, let's get things straight, once and for all. I lost my head last night. I was feeling sorry for myself for a lot of reasons. I walked into trouble at that saloon. I was like a kid who's been hurt and wants to hurt someone back. It's a mistake I'll not make again."

The lawyer blinked at him.

"I believe what you say about Dodsworth. I believe he probably saved my life by tossing me in here last night. I also believe that he would like nothing better than to see me ride out of this valley and not come back. Tom's grown old and fat and comfortable. He's stopped thinking. It's easier for him to take Jud Laws' orders."

Roberts said nothing.

"The town's the same way. Len Petrie used to be a man. At least, I thought he was. I had respect for him. But the man I knew, or thought I knew, no longer exists. He'd like to have me leave, too. He doesn't want me moving into court, bringing up the fact that the loan under which the Running R was foreclosed was not legal."

"He's human," said Roberts.

"Certainly, he's human. Well, he's going to get hurt. A lot of people in this valley are going to get hurt. I'm going to pick it up by its heels and shake it, until everyone who's taken a dollar or a favor from Jud Laws gets what's coming to him.

"Now clear out of here. Get hold of the judge and file whatever papers are necessary to set aside that foreclosure sale."

"He'll throw you out of court."

"That's what I want him to do. I want to take this to the state courts, and if necessary, to the governor. Let's get started."

"And what happens if I do? They'll take you before the judge and get you six to eight months for disturbing the peace, or attempted murder, or anything they happen to think of at the moment. How are you going to go to the governor then?"

"I'll find a way."

"Sure," Roberts snorted. "The world is full of suckers who thought they could beat the game. And who got hurt? They did."

"Are you going to file those papers?"

"If that's what you want. But I still think you'd better ride out. Every friend you have in this town would tell you the same."

"I haven't any friend in this town." Reynolds stopped, his eyes touching the tray of dirty breakfast dishes. "I'm wrong. I have one friend: Jenny Hay. She's a strange little girl."

The lawyer shrugged. After he had gone, Reynolds sat again on the bunk, considering what the lawyer had said. Everyone seemed to be trying to get him to leave town. He could understand Jud Laws having him killed. He was a threat to the rancher so long as he remained. But what good would it do Jud to put him behind bars for six to eight months? As soon as he got out he would start over, and Laws must know this.

What was going to happen in the next few months that might change the picture?

He had part of his answer in the middle of the afternoon, for the sheriff himself came to the cell door, rattling the keys.

"You've got a visitor."

There was no one he could think of that Reynolds wanted to see. Jenny had brought him a sandwich and more coffee at noon, and this time he had tried to talk to her, but she only left the food, picked up the breakfast tray, and went in silence through the cell door.

"Who is it?"

"Miss Belle Carstairs."

Reynolds shook his head. "You must have the wrong cell, Sheriff. I never heard of a Belle Carstairs."

Dodsworth paid him no attention. He unlocked the door and stood aside.

"I hate to have you come into this place, miss," he said to the girl Reynolds could not yet see because of the turn in the passage. "Wouldn't you rather talk to him in the office?"

Her voice was low and throaty, the accent telling plainly that she was not from that part of the country. "I want to talk to him alone."

The sheriff grumbled. She walked past him into the cell, and in spite of himself, Boyd Reynolds caught his breath. She was the most beautiful woman he had ever seen.

It was hard to guess her age, but he thought she must be in her mid-twenties. Her hair was a red gold, but it had a body that Ellen Petrie's had never had, and her clothes were rich and highly styled. He had seen women dressed in similar fashion in front of the Palace Hotel in San Francisco, or going to the American Theater, but no-where else.

He came to his feet without thought, glad suddenly that he had put on the clean shirt and that he had shaved.

"You wanted to see me?"

Her eyes were a hazel brown. It was hard to tell. They seemed to change color as she turned away from the window light to look at him.

"If you are Boyd Reynolds."

"I'm Reynolds."

She surveyed the cell with obvious distaste. He waited until Dodsworth had locked the door and gone with heavy steps back along the corridor, then he said, "The only place to sit is on the bunk."

She glanced at the bare pad, but made no move to accept the invitation.

"I'm Belle Carstairs." She had a direct way of speaking which he liked, a way of looking directly at him while she talked.

He said, "I'm sorry. The name doesn't mean anything to me."

Her eyes lifted in surprise. "I own the TC. Rather, my family does."

He started, then his mouth quirked sardonically. He had been impressed by her appearance, and good-looking women had always had the power to move him, but those few words had killed whatever interest he might have had in her.

She was an enemy, and the cold, hard rage that gripped him knew no compromise. She might look like an angel, but she was still the one he had to fight.

"I am honored." He made her a little bow.

It surprised her, and she looked at him with more attention. Belle Carstairs had been raised in a world that knew form and convention and honored them, a world that seldom came into direct contact with the raw edge of reality.

This, she recognized, was a savage land, populated with people who by her standards were less than civilized. The country had appalled her by its vastness, by its rugged mountains and snow-capped peaks.

The town, with its unpaved streets, its unpainted houses, its saloons and dusty store, was as foreign to her as would have been the wasteland of the moon.

And she realized suddenly that this man facing her was someone beyond her experience. There was something very

49

vital and compelling about him, for all that his face was battered, scarred by the fight, that his dark hair needed cutting and that the shirt, although fresh, was worn, frayed at the collar.

"I am glad you feel honored." She had recovered her poise in that single instant, and her sarcasm matched his. "I suppose you are not accustomed to your victims coming to you to beg?"

"Victims?" He did not understand.

"Victims," Her voice was steady. "I do not pretend to comprehend this country or its legal processes. In England if a robber is in jail we assume that he will be duly punished, and some effort will be made to return our property. But here it appears to be different."

"You know," said Reynolds, "I have a nagging suspicion that you and I are not walking on the same side of the street, that we are at cross-purposes. Are you saying that I stole something from you?"

"Do you deny it? I thought it was common knowledge in this valley that you and your men have consistently raided the TC, running off our cattle and killing our crew."

Reynolds began to laugh. There was no humor in him, only bitter irony. That he who had lost everything at the hands of the big cattle company should be accused by it of stealing . . .

"I said we weren't talking the same language." His tone was rough. "I don't know what you've been told, or who told you—although it's fairly obvious that it was Jud Laws —but whoever it was is the greatest liar unhung."

"I, of course, expected you to say that."

"Did you?" he asked. "Then why did you trouble to come?"

She took a full minute before answering. "I am a direct person, Reynolds. I don't pretend to know anything about business, and I'm not used to handling it, but at the moment I have no choice."

He did not answer, and after a moment she went on. "If I had had anything to say about it, we would never have invested in this cattle company. It's too far from England, and none of us knows much about it."

50

"Then why did you?"

She moved her hands a little. "Parkhurst talked my uncle into it. Parkhurst knew ranching. Then my uncle died and my father inherited. My father is an invalid. He cannot move without a wheel chair."

"I'm sorry."

"I don't know why I'm telling you this. I certainly had no intention of telling you when I came here—anyhow, after Parkhurst had his accident things went from bad to worse, apparently. My father sent me out to see what could be done. We have received no revenue from the ranch for over a year."

Reynolds said, "And what did you expect to accomplish, coming to me?"

"I don't really know." She sounded puzzled. She *was* puzzled. Why had she come? She thought about it carefully. "I guess I came out of desperation. When I arrived in Colorado I had the naïve idea that there would be a certain amount of law to help me. I had a letter to the governor. I went to Denver and saw him. He appointed a commissioner to investigate, and we came up here together.

"We talked to Mr. Laws and the man at the bank and the sheriff. They all told us the outlaws were out of hand, that they could not control them, could not protect our cattle. The state has no force which can, or will, act. We appear helpless to combat you."

"You believe all of that?"

She met his eyes directly. "I did until I saw you."

"And now?"

"I don't know."

He considered. "Just what did you expect to gain by talking to me?"

Again she spread her hands slightly. "I honestly am not quite certain. I spent part of the winter in southern Italy, two years ago. I have relatives with estates in Sicily. Over there they pay tribute to the local bandits to protect their property. I suppose that is what I had in mind, to arrange a yearly fee for you and your men to leave us alone."

Reynolds hid a tight smile. "Did Jud Laws know you intended doing this?"

"No."

"Does he know you've come to see me?"

"No."

"He will. The sheriff or one of his deputies will see to that. There's precious little that goes on in Hunt Valley that Jud Laws doesn't know about, soon."

She was staring at him now. "I do not understand."

"No," he said, "I don't think you do. Nor do I expect you to believe me. I assume you have been telling the truth as you see it. Now let me tell you a couple of things. You can believe me or not, as you choose.

"First, I have been away. I have just come home from three years of wandering. When I left here there were twenty small outfits in the valley, including the Running R, which was owned by my brother and myself. Today the TC is the only outfit in the valley. Every other one has been swallowed up. If you want the records, go to the courthouse.

"Second, my brother was murdered. So were several others who dared stand against Jud Laws. I have no doubt that your ranch is losing cattle. But if you want to know what's happened to them, ask Jud Laws. He knows far better than anyone else."

She looked at him for a full moment of silence, then without another word to him, she turned to the door, raising her voice.

"Sheriff, I am ready to leave."

CHAPTER SIX

JENNY HAY crossed the hotel lobby toward the street door. Her father looked up from his place behind the desk, his usually placid face showing concern.

"Where are you going?"

"To pick up the dishes at the jail."

"Jenny," he said softly, "come here."

She retraced her steps slowly. There was a deep bond between these two, heightened by Dan Hay's awareness that somewhere along the road he had failed.

He had started out with high hopes, fifteen years ago, when after his wife's death he had brought his tiny daughter to Kernville and opened this hotel.

Before that he had been a gambler, a rather successful gambler. But on the night his wife died, help had failed to reach her in time because he was sitting at a card table in a Denver saloon.

He had never touched a card again. He had come to Kernville to get away from the men with whom he had been associated through the years, and he had resolved to spend the rest of his life making up to Jenny for the loss of her mother.

"You'll get yourself talked about." His voice was gentle, not chiding. "It's no good, Jenny. You can't help him. No one can."

She was looking at him steadily. "I've got to, Dad. I simply have to do what I can."

"Why? What is he to you?"

She shook her head. "He doesn't know I'm alive. He was always in love with Ellen Petrie. I used to watch him at the dances. And I used to hear her discuss him with the other girls."

"Then, why?"

"He's so alone—I hate this town. I hate the way Jud Laws lords it over all of you. I hate the way the men knuckle under to him."

Her father sighed. "I know. Laws is a bad one. I've known his kind, a lot of them. But, Jenny, they are the people who get what they want in this world. Because others are too good or too decent, or merely too weak to stand against them."

She gave him a long look. Then she went quietly from the lobby, stepping out into the afternoon sun.

In the jail office one of the deputies smirked at her. "Taking good care of him, ain't you?"

She ignored him. The man had his feet on the desk. He made no effort to rise. The keys hung from a nail, over which the big ring had been slipped. She took them down and moved along the hall to the cell door.

Reynolds was pacing back and forth inside like a caged cat. He swung around as she unlocked the door, and came forward quickly to grasp her arm.

"Jenny. Do me a favor, will you?"

She stood startled, then she nodded.

"Find Bolger Roberts and send him over here."

"If he's sober."

"If he isn't, sober him up. This is important."

She nodded again, to say she understood. "Did you have enough to eat?"

He made an impatient gesture. "Sure, of course. But hurry and get Roberts."

She gathered up the dishes, moved to the door, locked it after her and left the building. Her thoughts were bitter as she went back to the hotel, and her father saw her face as she crossed the lobby.

"What's the matter, honey?"

"Nothing," she said. "Nothing at all."

She took the dishes on to the kitchen. When she came back her father was still at the desk.

"Did Reynolds say something to upset you?"

"He practically didn't say anything at all. He simply does not know I exist. All I'm good for is to bring him coffee and food and run errands for him."

"What kind of errands?" Her father's voice quickened.

"Just that he wants to see his lawyer."

"I see. You know the English girl who's staying here?"

"The TC woman? Yes."

"She went to the jail this afternoon—to see Reynolds."

His daughter stopped, thinking about this, picturing in her mind's eye the older girl, her beauty, the expensive clothes. "So that's what upset him." She said it half under her breath. "He was ready to climb the walls—I've got to find Roberts."

Twenty minutes later the lawyer presented himself at

the jail. To Reynolds' surprise, he was sober, although shaky.

"Jenny said you wanted to see me."

In a low voice Boyd told him about Belle Carstairs' visit. "Laws told her and the governor's commissioner that the hill people and I have been raiding the TC herd. Now she doesn't know what to believe."

Roberts shrugged. "You can't blame her. A lot of the cattle are missing."

"Where are they?"

Roberts shrugged again. "No one knows. They were started for the railroad. A lot of them never got there. You know this country. Where would you guess they went?"

Reynolds thought about it carefully. "The only pass you could get any number of cattle over, except the main one, is through Death Canyon. But that's a rough trail."

"Maybe not too rough for Laws."

"So Laws wants to keep me cooped up here while he rounds up what's left of the TC animals and steals most of them."

Roberts sighed. "I wouldn't worry about that if I were you. The Carstairs' troubles aren't your business. You've got trouble enough as it is. Judge Dixon threw me out of court when I tried to have the sale of the Running R set aside."

"What do you mean, it isn't my business? Some of those cattle are Running R stock. I've got to get out of here."

"Escape? Now wait a minute—" Bolger Roberts was as near excitement as Boyd had ever seen him. "You can't do that. You'd ruin everything."

"Ruin what?" His client had been stalking up and down the small cell. He stopped, swinging around to face the lawyer. "What is there to ruin? While I sit here and twist my fingers Laws will be on his way with the cattle. When I get out, all any of us will have left is empty land."

"Look. I've already appealed to the state courts. I wrote a letter to the governor this morning. Maybe we can get an injunction to keep Laws from shipping until we have the hearing."

"Do you believe that?"

Roberts' face showed that he did not.

"I tell you, I have to get out. You rent a horse and ride up to the Crossing. Most of the buildings burned the other night, but Alf Bentley and the rest are camped up there, waiting to hear from me."

"But, Boyd—"

"Do as I tell you. It's too late today for you to get them back here tonight. Tell them to make it tomorrow night. A few of them can start shooting up the other end of town. When the sheriff and his men run up to see what the ruckus is all about, someone can loop a rope around those bars and yank out that window. It's only spiked into the frame."

Bolger whined. "Man, it's near forty miles to the canyon. I haven't ridden that far in thirty years."

"Do you good. Shake some of the whiskey out of you. Now get going."

The lawyer looked at him despairingly; then, as if realizing the futility of argument, he sighed, turned toward the door, and called for the deputy.

An hour later Max Cleaver, standing in the doorway of the Paradise saloon with Jud Laws, turned his head as Bolger Roberts rode out.

He watched until the lawyer dropped down the grade and took the northern trail.

"Where do you suppose he's going? I haven't seen him in a saddle since I came here."

"I don't know," Laws' mind was on something else. "That damned English dame. She went to see Reynolds at the jail. God knows what he told her."

"We'd better start rounding up the herd. I don't like the governor sending that investigator down."

"I don't either. You can tell the boys to start in the morning."

Cleaver was still looking after the departing lawyer, now little more than a dot on the distant trail.

"Just for kicks I'm going to send a rider after Roberts and see what the old drunk is up to." He turned and poked his head into the saloon. "Hey, Ernie. I've got a job for you."

Bolger Roberts did not realize he was being followed. He was too occupied with the painfulness of staying on the horse to even consider the possibility. Before he had covered five miles it seemed to him that every nerve in his body was being punctured with hot needles. Twice he stopped, debating turning around and heading back to town.

"How'd I get involved in all this?" He said it aloud. "What does Boyd Reynolds and his ranch and his crazy notion of fighting Jud Laws mean to me? I'm through and I know it. Why do I keep struggling to pretend that I'm still a human being?"

But he rode on. At dark he pulled off the trail, not wishing to be discovered by any riders drifting in from the TC's northern line camp, and made a fireless camp, carefully hobbling the rented horse before he drew the bottle from his pocket and pulled the cork.

Within five minutes he was snoring raggedly, unaware that Cleaver's man was less than a thousand yards from him in a small, timbered draw, cursing the fact that he had ridden out without supplies.

In the morning Roberts lifted himself stiffly into the saddle and continued north, swinging wide of the old Running R buildings, and so came into the canyon's mouth. He rode on up the twisting trail at a steady gait. He had not been up this way in years, but he had had many good times at the Crossing in times past, and the memories brought a smile to his lips.

Alf will drop dead when he sees me, he thought. *Alf won't believe I can ride this far.*

Alf Bentley did not drop dead when he saw Roberts ride past the gutted frames of the burned buildings. Despite his fat, Alf Bentley was a durable man. Yet as he walked out of the rubbish they were combing for salvage, he was surprised.

"You're a long way from home, Bolger."

The lawyer climbed down gingerly and stood for a moment testing his legs, one and then the other, in an effort to prove to himself that they still worked.

"So I am. Boyd Reynolds sent you a message."

At once the attitude of the men, who had gathered around him, changed, sharpened.

Bentley said, "What's happened to him? Why didn't he come himself?"

"He's in jail," Roberts said flatly. "And he wants you to get him out." He gave them the story.

Bentley swore. "I might have known. Some of the boys figured he'd run out, and others claimed he must have made a deal with Jud Laws."

Roberts laughed heavily. "You don't know Boyd if you believe like that. In fact, I'm not sure any of us knows him. He's changed a lot, seems overnight. When he was a kid he'd do about anything for anyone, and he'd go a long way out of his path to keep from hurting anybody. That time's past. He's poison mean now."

Slim Maynard said to Bentley, "How do we know this whiskey pot is telling it straight? For a bottle of red-eye he'd ride out here with any story Laws wanted to send. This could be a trap."

Roberts looked around at the circle of men watching him. There were eighteen, not counting Bentley, and it came to the lawyer that he had never seen as case-hardened a crew. If they failed to believe him he had no doubt that someone of them would slit his throat and drop him down one of the caving mine shafts.

He shrugged. "Do what you want. Boyd sent the message, no matter what you think. If I'm lying, the only way you'll find out is to ride in and see."

"I believe him," Bentley said. "Don't ask me why—maybe because if he'd taken a bottle from Laws I think he'd have stopped on the far side of the first hill, drained it, and then ridden on back. Anyhow, I'm going in. This is the only chance we have. If we don't move against Laws now, we might as well high-tail it across the hills and pull clear out of the country."

There was a grumbled assent from the others. Maynard said reluctantly, "All right, I'll go along. But Roberts rides with us. And the first sign I see of a double cross, he gets a bullet in his back."

The lawyer moaned. "I don't mind getting shot, but I

just can't face another forty miles of riding right now.
I just can't."

"Sure, you can." Alf Bentley was unbending. "Catch
him up a fresh horse, Tom. The rest of you get saddled."
He looked at the lawyer without pity. "I know it's tough
on you, but it's either ride now or never ride out of here.
We've gone too far, and most of us have lost too much,
to take a chance with anyone."

"All right," said Roberts. "All right! But for God sake,
let me take a bottle along."

CHAPTER SEVEN

MAX CLEAVER was just sitting down to dinner in the Har-
mond Restaurant when he saw Ernie Haws ride in. He left
the table at once and, stepping out onto the board sidewalk,
walked along it to where Haws was tethering his horse at
the rail before the Paradise saloon.

"Did you follow Roberts?"

Haws turned. His bearded cheeks were covered with dust
turned blackish by dried sweat. "I did. Clear to the Crossing."

"So that's were he went."

"That's where he went. And they're all riding in. They
aren't more than half an hour behind me."

Cleaver fished in his pocket and found a silver dollar.
"Buy yourself a drink. Tell the boys in the saloon to round
up any of the rest of the crew that are in town. I want them
to meet me at the livery corral in ten minutes."

He turned away and moved quickly down the street.
Haws rubbed his lantern jaw reflectively; then, flipping the
silver dollar into the air, he went into the saloon. He was
grinning when he came against the bar. Mav Cleaver seldom
bought a drink for anyone. He must, Haws thought, be
thoroughly pleased.

Cleaver was pleased. His long legs carried him down the side street to the gate of Leonard Petrie's house, where he turned in.

When Ellen answered his knock he said, "Hate to trouble you, Ellen, but is Jud here?"

She looked at him, hesitating. There was little love lost between her and Laws' foreman. "We're just sitting down to supper."

"Sorry." His tone held no apology. Max Cleaver seldom apologized to anyone, never to a woman. "This is important."

She shrugged, then moved back into the hall, leaving the door ajar. A moment later Jud appeared.

"What is it?"

"Ernie Haws just rode back. Bentley's bringing his full crew in to bust Reynolds out of jail."

Jud Laws started to laugh. "They are, huh? I'll be right with you." He turned into the house, then reappeared, carrying his hat.

Ellen followed him onto the porch. "Jud, what is it? Do you really have to go?"

"Have to," he said. "The hill people are causing trouble again." He kissed her briefly, then hurried down the walk to overtake Cleaver.

Cleaver glanced back once and saw that the girl was still on the porch, staring after them. He grunted.

"Got you saddle broke, ain't she?"

Laws glanced at him. "Your business?"

"It's my business if it intereferes with things. I never yet seen a woman that wasn't trouble. Cut and run while you can."

"Maybe I like it."

"Talk around town is that she was sweet for Reynolds until you put the squeeze on the old man at the bank."

Dull red came up under Jud's heavy tan, and Cleaver did not miss the sign. "There's too much talk. And you do too much listening."

"That's the way I learn things. She's playing you for a sucker, Jud. Did she ever give you a tumble before her father lost his shirt in the cattle deal?"

"All right," said Laws. "All right. I want her. Can you understand that?"

Cleaver was silent.

"Don't worry, I'll handle her. Now, what do you plan for Bentley?"

"Spread the boys out and blast them as they come into town."

"No."

"Why not?"

"Because they'll never get near the jail that way. I want them to get to the jail. I want Boyd Reynolds to break out. I don't want him sitting safe in that cell while Bentley's crowd are mowed down. I want him dead, too."

Cleaver grinned. "I hadn't thought of that."

"The difference between you and me," Jud Laws said coldly, "is that I think. You charge ahead blindly, like a bull. Think with your head, friend, not with a gun. Now, don't tell the sheriff anything. You never know what that fool Dodsworth will do. He might even try to stop it. He's got some silly ideas about not having killings inside his town.

"Get the boys strung out around the courthouse and on the roofs of the other buildings, then wait. You fire the first shot. And you don't fire until you see Boyd Reynolds on the street. Then make certain you hit him."

Without further word he turned around and headed back for the Petrie house and his waiting supper.

Max Cleaver watched him go. A violent man, Cleaver had been at odds with the world almost since first memory. He had run away from his Texas home at eleven, joining a northbound trail herd. He had killed his first man at seventeen, ridden by the uncontrollable temper which was his principal weakness.

Not until he had met Jud Laws had his life known any real purpose. He had been a gambler, a shotgun messenger, a range detective, and bounty hunter. Always his gun had been for hire in one way or another. The idea of owning anything had not occurred to him until two years before, when he signed up with the TC.

He and Laws had sized each other up at their first meeting, and it was to Cleaver that Laws had first unfolded his dream of a huge ranch north of Encampment, in Wyoming, to be stocked with TC beef.

The ranch was in Cleaver's name, but theirs was a partnership unwritten but binding, for they needed each other, and both were fully aware of the fact.

Laws was the brains. Cleaver had recognized this from the beginning, but Laws was also a physical coward. Cleaver knew this, and it gave him a sense of power. The fact that Laws had turned back to the shelter of Petrie's house while he moved up the street to face the battle with Bentley's men neither surprised nor distressed him.

There was an animal cunning in Max Cleaver, and a sadistic urge to see people hurt. Jud Laws had none of this. He killed for one reason and one only: profit. There was only the single area of disagreement between them: Ellen Petrie. Cleaver did not trust womankind. He had no use for them, and he was ruthless where they were concerned. The idea that any man could allow himself to become a slave to a woman because of desire was beyond his comprehension.

He would have to do something about Ellen Petrie, that he knew, and his mind worried the idea as he strode on toward the corral.

He placed his men carefully, encircling the jail. For himself he chose a spot on the roof of the blacksmith shop, directly covering the barred jail window. Then he sat down to wait.

From where he sat he could just barely see the top of Reynolds' head as the prisoner sat on the bunk against the cell wall.

Boyd had been sitting there for a full hour, champing at the inactivity. He watched the darkness deepen outside the window, and made no effort to light the lamp in the wall bracket of the cell.

He waited for the sound of firing from the north end of town. That would be the signal to draw the sheriff and his deputies away from the office, the signal that someone would throw a rope through the window bars and jerk them from their wooden frame.

The firing came at last. He jumped up, rushing to the window. He heard the rush of feet as Dodsworth and his men dashed out into the darkness before the courthouse. Then he waited again, the minutes ticking off in his head as if it were a clock.

Outside, a flurry of hoofs sounded, and he saw two dark horsemen ride toward him through the gloom. The leader pulled his animal up sharply, and a rope end flipped between the bars.

Reynolds caught it and snaked it around the uprights. "All right." His yell filled the night.

He saw the horseman swing about, saw him jump his animal forward. The rope tightened, its far end snubbed around the high horn of the rider's saddle, and for an instant the horse was yanked almost to a stop.

Then the wood holding the bars split with a crashing sound and the animal charged across the street.

Reynolds went through the opening like a cat slipping from a confining bag. He landed on his hands and knees, and this probably saved his life. Cleaver's gun blasted from the opposite roof. The bullet smashed into the jail wall just above Boyd's head.

Reynolds went flat, cursing as the guns opened up all around the street.

One of the riders who had come to his rescue went down. The other drove spurs to his horse, diving for the shelter of the side street.

On his belly, squirming like a snake, Reynolds worked his way toward the corner of the building. The gun across from him was still hammering, its bullets kicking up dirt around him.

Cleaver had come to his feet, the better to see. His big body was clearly outlined against the lighter sky. But the deep shadow along the foot of the jail wall screened Reynolds, and he heard Cleaver's voice run sharply through the night.

"He's somewhere in the courthouse yard. Don't let him get away."

The yell acted as a spur. Reynolds reached the rear corner of the jail and scrambled around it. He paused for

63

an instant, on hands and knees, breathing heavily, trying to collect his thoughts.

It had been a trap. That much was plain. He wondered if Bolger Roberts had betrayed the plan. Then he decided against this, for most of Bentley's men had not ridden far into town; they had paused at the north end, as he had directed, their shots pulling the sheriff from the jail.

Only two of the hill men had ridden in, and one of them was down. If the whole bunch had come this far the slaughter would have been terrible.

The shooting had stopped, and he guessed that the men who had been on the roofs must be working their way to the ground. He had only a moment's respite, unless he wanted to be hemmed in.

He debated. The impulse was to leap to his feet and run for the straggling row of single-storied buildings which marked the southern limit of the town.

But he would be in the open from the instant he left the jail wall. Better to round the building to the alley and try to make his way along that until he could find a hiding place.

There was no sound from the north. That probably meant that Bentley's crew had pulled out. He came to his feet and started along the rear of the jail. Behind him he heard the confused babble of shouts as Cleaver redirected his men.

Boyd Reynolds began to run. The alley ahead of him was littered with rubbish of all kinds. Twice he stumbled over some unseen object and went down into the soft sand. He was thankful for the heavy darkness, even though it made it nearly impossible to see where he was going.

Steps sounded around the corner of the jail, and a shout rang after him. "The alley. Watch the alley. He had to go that way."

Boyd redoubled his speed, casting all caution to the wind. He covered one block and then dashed across the side street. From his right he heard a shot and then a yell.

"There he goes."

A gun fired from the corner of the main street beside

64

the Paradise, the bullet smacking into the building at the corner of the alley even as Reynolds dove past it.

Feet raced along the sidewalk of the street he had just crossed. Other men were coming up the alley at a half run. And then ahead of him he saw something move. He ducked sidewise, brushing against a board fence. He reached up, grabbed its top, which was level with his shoulders, and half vaulted, half fell into the yard beyond.

Again he landed on all fours. Then he was up, running toward the rear of the building that loomed ahead, realizing that it was the hotel.

The rear door opened into a dark kitchen. He closed it behind him carefully, pausing to listen. He could hear no sound inside, but from the alley he had just exited there came an indistinct jumble of shouts. They had lost him, but he knew it was only a matter of time until they would search every building on the block.

He stole cross the dark kitchen. A wide door gave into the dining room and he cracked it to peer through. The space beyond was in semidarkness, illuminated by a trickle of light from the lobby entrance.

Excited voices reached him from the street out front and he retreated to the big, square kitchen, fumbling around its walls, searching for a place of concealment.

He opened one door and then another. The first led into a pantry, the second was a closet. Then the third disclosed a steep flight of stairs leading upward.

He closed the door after him and fumbled for the treads in pitch blackness. They were so steep, he had the sensation of climbing a ladder.

His groping hands felt the landing at the top, and he paused before the solid door there. A thread of light told him a lamp was burning in the hall, and he put his ear against the panel, listening intently.

He heard no sound of movement and tried the door gently. It was unlocked. He eased it open and peered out. The upper hall was empty.

He stepped into it and moved along it swiftly, gaining his own room. Inside, he paused again, putting his back to the jamb, breathing deeply, hearing the throb of his racing pulse hammer in his ears.

His bed roll lay on the chair, partly open, where Jenny had found his clean shirt and socks. A little light came through the window, enough to show him his way. He fumbled through the roll, then drew a deep breath of relief as he found his spare gun. He thrust it under his belt and shifted his attention to the window.

This looked out on a vacant lot and across that to the street. In the east the moon was coming up slowly, sending its yellow glow across the town.

Men moved on the street and he swore under his breath. There was no escape in that direction. He turned back toward the hall, looking its full length before venturing into it.

He moved down it to the back, looking out of the window there at the littered yard and the alley beyond, being careful not to show himself in the bright rectangle.

There were men in the alley now, and he shrank back against the wall. The town was alive with TC riders, and they would never quit until they ran him down. He hesitated. If he could somehow climb to the hotel's flat roof he might be able to escape detection when they searched the building.

He turned back along the hall and had traveled more than half its length when the door on his right swung open. He froze, his hand darting to the heavy gun, pulling it free as he turned. Then he stopped, for Jenny Hay was staring out at him from the dark room.

"Boyd." Her voice was very loud with surprise.

He said, "Shhh . . ." and she dropped her tone to a whisper.

"That shooting. It was you they were shooting at?"

He nodded.

"I didn't know. The TC men hurrah the place so often that none of us pays much attention any more. How'd you get away?"

He told her quickly.

"And how are you going to get out of here?"

That he did not know. "If I can get to a horse—" He

66

became aware that she was wearing a robe over a long nightdress. He had been too concerned with his own problems to give such attention to anything else.

"If I could get to the roof—"

"There's a trap door from Father's room, but you need a ladder, and what good would the roof do you? You can't get down from it."

"I've got to get out somehow. They'll be searching all the buildings—"

He broke off, for suddenly there were loud voices from the lobby below, and he recognized Max Cleaver's tones.

"Reynolds come through here?"

Dan Hay said, "Reynolds? I thought he was in jail."

Cleaver's voice was tight. "He broke out, and went up the alley. If you're lying—"

"I never thought it necessary to lie to anyone." Dan Hay's voice had a flat sound. "And I am not about ready to start now."

The girl and Boyd exchanged quick glances.

Cleaver said, "Who's upstairs?"

"My daughter and the English girl. They've both gone to bed."

"Is there a back stairway?"

"There is, from the kitchen."

"All right. Ernie, you cover the kitchen. The rest of you come on. We'll search the place. He probably came in from the alley."

Hay's voice was suddenly tense. "You aren't the sheriff, Cleaver, and I haven't seen a search warrant. No one goes through my place, disturbing my guests, even if they work for TC."

There was the quick sound of a sharp blow, and the thud as someone fell. Jenny's mouth opened as if to cry out, but she made no sound.

Cleaver said hashly, "I've heard about you, Hay. I heard you were a gambler once, and that you were a little fancy with a gun. You want to try it?"

There was a murmur which Boyd and the girl could not distinguish, then Cleaver laughed.

"That's what I thought. You tinhorns are all alike. Don't

you ever tell me what I can or can't do, not unless you want to see how fast you are. See if he's got a gun, Shorty."

There was a moment of silence, then a gruff voice said, "He's clean."

"Okay. Watch him. The rest of you come on upstairs. What room is the Carstairs woman in?"

"One."

"Don't bother her, boys. Jud's got trouble enough with her already. And I don't think she'll have Reynolds under her bed." He laughed heavily, and there was the sound of boots crossing the floor and starting up the steps.

Jenny grabbed Reynolds' arm. She pulled him into her room and shut the door, sliding the bolt into place.

He whispered, "If they find the bolt thrown they'll know I'm in here and break the door down."

"Get into bed."

The only light in the room was the faint glow that drifted in from the window. He stared at her.

"Get in the bed, quick," she repeated urgently.

It was a double bed, its side shoved against the outside wall. Reynolds threw back the heavy covers and crawled in, crowding back until his body was against the wall, depressed into the crack between bed and wall. He heard her slide the bolt open again, then she leaped quietly across the room and into the bed.

She turned her back to him, pressing herself against him until both of them occupied only the far side of the mattress.

"Get your head under the pillow and don't make a sound, no matter what happens. Don't move."

He would have protested, but already he could hear the tramp of boots in the hall outside. He crouched down beneath the covers in the narrow space between her warm body and the wall, his head under the pillow. He knew what she was trying to do—to make it appear that she was alone in the double bed.

The door banged open suddenly and the girl beside him screamed. She came up on one elbow, the covers about her shoulders blocking any view of him from the hall.

"Who is it? What is it? Father! Father!" she was yelling loudly.

"Shut up." It was Cleaver's voice. "Stop that racket."

A woman's voice took up the cry from the far end of the corridor. "Mr. Hay. Mr. Hay. What's happening? Are we all to be murdered in our beds?"

Cleaver said hoarsely, "There goes the damned English woman." He disappeared from the doorway. "It's all right, Miss Carstairs. A man broke jail and we're looking for him."

"What man?"

"Boyd Reynolds. You'd better pray that we find him. If we don't, half the cattle you've got left will be gone in a month."

"How did he escape?" From where Boyd lay, his ears muffled by the thick covers, it was hard to tell, but he thought she must have come into the hall.

At least she was distracting Cleaver's attention. Boyd lay half smothered, gripping the handle of his gun. If they discovered him he would shoot his way out. There were probably too many for him to get them all, but he was not going to be taken alive.

Belle Carstairs was saying, "What are you men doing in Miss Hay's door?" Her tone was shocked, and Boyd knew she had come up to them. Her sarcasm grew. "Surely you don't think he is hiding in Miss Hay's bed?"

Boyd had a sudden insane impulse to laugh. He choked his mouth full of the covers, feeling Jenny's warm body jerk convulsively, and knew that she, too, was having difficulty containing her laughter.

Cleaver was mumbling something he could not hear.

"You do work for the TC, don't you?" The English girl's voice had sharpened with authority.

"Why, yes." The question caught Cleaver by surprise.

"Very well. I own the TC, and I certainly do not approve of my employees racing around, firing off their guns and breaking into people's hotels. What is your name?"

Boyd Reynolds would have loved to see Max Cleaver's face. He felt confident that no one had ever talked to Cleaver in this tone or in this manner.

The answer came grudgingly. "Max Cleaver."

"And you work for me? I order you to get out of here as fast as you can. I will report your conduct to Mr. Laws in the morning."

"But—we've got to find Reynolds."

"That is a job for the sheriff. I assume that you have not been deputized?"

Cleaver snorted, then said to his men, "Search the rest of the rooms. Hers, too. He's got to be here somewhere."

The feet tramped along the hall. The sound of doors being opened and closed came back to Reynolds. He heard Belle Carstairs gasp, then she said to Jenny Hay, "I am going to report this to the sheriff, right away."

"Don't bother," Jenny told her.

She had twisted to sit up in the bed, the covers hugged up around her small shoulders, thus making a kind of tent under which Boyd lay. She reached over and raised the blankets a little, and he knew that she did this to give him a breath of air.

The other girl was still there, saying, "I don't understand. You say not to bother—men come crashing into your room and you can say don't bother?"

Jenny told her tightly, "I mean, don't bother to tell Dodsworth. He isn't going to do anything, Miss Carstairs. No one is going to do anything. He takes his orders from Jud Laws. And Max Cleaver and his men take their orders from Jud. They wouldn't be here unless Jud told them to be. They've got only one thing in mind, to kill Boyd Reynolds."

"To kill him? You mean murder?"

"They won't call it that. They'll say he was killed trying to escape from jail. But he'll be just as dead."

"Why . . . why this is unbelievable . . ."

Jenny's voice softened a little. "Miss Carstairs, I know you're not used to our country or our ways. I am not defending the sheriff, or Cleaver, and certainly not Jud Laws. And I have no use for the townspeople who have knuckled under to them. Most of them did it in the hope of profit. But the fact remains that a lot of the blame rests on you and your family."

"On me? On my family?"

"That's right. You put up the money to buy the TC. Parkhurst came over here and bought up one ranch after another in the valley. As long as he was running it, things weren't so bad. But after he was killed and Jud took over, the little ranchers got squeezed out. Some of them were deliberately killed. Others were driven away."

"But we knew nothing about that."

"Whose fault? There is responsibility connected with ownership, Miss Carstairs. You never even started to ask questions; you never worried at all until your profits stopped. Isn't that true?"

The other girl had moved into the room. "I guess it is . . . but . . ."

"I know, you didn't know. People died, and you didn't know."

"If what you say is true, I'll fire Jud in the morning."

"I'm afraid it isn't quite that simple any more. You still don't understand. Jud Laws is king of this valley. He couldn't be more powerful if the TC belonged to him outright. He owns the judge and the courts. He has thirty fighting men on his payroll, not regular cowhands, but murderers and outlaws. And as long as they work for Jud, they're safe and they know it."

"But surely the governor—"

"Is a long way off. There are no state police, and I can't see him calling the militia to put Jud off your ranch."

Belle Carstairs sank onto the edge of the bed. "Then what am I going to do?"

Jenny had no answer to that.

Cleaver tramped back into the doorway, saying grudgingly, "I guess he isn't here. But he won't get away. You can write that down."

He moved on down the hall and they heard the men's boots as they descended the stairs and crossed the lobby below.

Jenny let her breath out with relief, then said to the other girl. "They're gone, and I'm very tired. If you don't mind."

To her astonishment, Boyd Reynolds threw back the

covers and sat up. Belle Carstairs uttered a small cry, then was very quiet.

Jenny said tensely, "What did you do that for?"

Reynolds slid to the foot of the bed and swung his feet to the floor. "I'd have smothered if I'd stayed down there another minute. Besides, I think Miss Carstairs and I have something to talk about."

"But she's the TC. What if she tells them?"

"I don't think she will. I think she has had a convincing lesson tonight, more convincing than anything I could have said."

"But—"

"And we owe her something. If she hadn't appeared when she did, and rattled Cleaver, he would probably have searched this room thoroughly and found me. What about it, Miss Carstairs? Do you want to talk?"

She looked from the girl to Boyd, wide-eyed. "I—I don't know. After all, you are an escaped convict—"

His mouth quirked thinly. "I am not a convict. I have never been tried for anything. I was being held in the county jail for having started a fight in the Paradise saloon. I didn't start it, but that part does not matter. I have not been tried, and I would not have been tried. They want me out of their way, that's all."

"I don't—"

"You don't know what to do. You just said that. All right, I don't know what you want to do, but I'm going to tell you what will happen. Your being here has upset Jud more than anything else could have. Before you came he was taking his time. He was diverting most of the cattle, stealing them. Now he'll step up his operation. He'll strip the TC range of every head he can gather. He'll leave you with a lot of pasture and not a head of stock to graze it. He'll get them away from here, probably out of the state. Then, if you have the money, you can try to fight him through the courts to get them back. Only if you win, finally, the case will have vanished."

Belle Carstairs made a little moaning sound. "Mr. Laws said only this afternoon that since my family needs money the best thing would be to round up the stock and drive them to the railroad."

"They'll never reach the railroad. If they once go out of this valley you'll never see them again."

There was heavy silence in the room, broken suddenly by the sound of feet on the stairs.

CHAPTER EIGHT

REYNOLDS AND THE GIRLS looked toward the hall in quick consternation. Then Boyd leaped across the room and slid behind the half-open door, his gun in his hand.

The steps came quickly forward; he heard Jenny's gasp of relief.

"Father."

"You all right?" Dan Hay stormed into the room. "If Cleaver hurt you—if he laid—"

"I'm all right. Have they gone?"

"They've gone. They didn't find Reynolds—"

Boyd stepped into sight, thrusting his gun in its place under his belt. Hay swung around. "Where you been—?"

"No matter."

"You'll never get out of town alive. They've got men guarding every street."

"I'll get out." Boyd said it grimly. He did not add that he would get out if he had to shoot his way through the whole TC crew. "That isn't the most important thing at the moment. I want to talk to Miss Carstairs, and it would be as well if neither of you heard what was said."

He saw the hurt in Jenny's eyes and added hastily, "It isn't that I don't trust both of you. I do. But there's no need in your getting any more involved than you already are. The very fact that anyone knows me is enough to sign their death warrant now."

Dan Hay said, "Never mind, that. I've had enough of Cleaver tonight. If you need another hand—"

Reynolds shook his head. "You'll be more help in town, where you can let me know what's going on. I can't trust Roberts. Liquor means too much to him."

He turned to the English girl, but Hay cut in. "Seems to me that if we're to be any help we'd better know what's going on here."

Reynolds gave him a wry grin. "You win. I just didn't want to jeopardize either of you. Now, Miss Carstairs, who are you going to trust?"

She bit her lip, looking from one to the other of them, watching Jenny for a long moment. Finally her head went up, her small chin thrusting out. "I'll trust you, Mr. Reynolds. God help me if I'm wrong."

He hid his small smile. "Good. Then you've got a job ahead. The first thing tomorrow you try to stop Laws from rounding up your cattle. I don't believe you can, but try. What we need is time. Roberts is trying to set aside the sale of the Running R to the TC in the courts, because the ranch was foreclosed on a mortgage that I did not sign. If we can get Laws into the state courts, and can bring you in as owner of the TC, it will strengthen our case. But it will do no good to recover title to cattle that are already gone."

"Do you think he will listen to me?"

Reynolds shook his head.

"Then what good will it do for me to ask?"

"Do it before witnesses, as many witnesses as possible. Then fire him and tell him you've hired me as manager of TC."

He saw suspicion leap into her eyes and he grinned tightly. "Laws told you I was head of an outlaw gang, didn't he? And you're afraid that now I'll steal you blind. I'll tell you this: you'll only be legalizing what I am going to do anyhow. I'm going to smash Laws and his fighting men. I'm going to recover the cattle that have been stolen from the little ranchers, including myself. And I'm going to get back as many TC animals for you as I can.

"If you believe that, do one other thing—no, two: take

74

Laws and his men off the payroll; and have Bolger Roberts serve Len Petrie, at the bank, with a letter stating that Laws is no longer in your employ and that his authority to draw TC funds is revoked."

She was silent for long moments. "All right. I'll do it. But I must warn you, Mr. Reynolds, I have no money to pay you or whatever men you employ."

"We'll worry about that later," he told her. "Dan, get some paper and a pen." As Hay turned out of the doorway, he went on. "Next, I have to get out of town and find my men."

"I wonder if you can," said Jenny. "After what happened here tonight they may have ridden clear out of the country."

"Not Alf Bentley." Boyd was confident. "The only way Alf will leave this territory is in a box. The Crossing is his home. It may be burned out, but the boys know they're safe in those hills."

Dan returned with the writing material and Belle Carstairs wrote the letter at Boyd's dictation. Dan Hay signed as witness. Reynolds then handed the paper to Jenny.

"I want this mailed to the governor of Colorado, tomorrow. Can you do that?"

She nodded and he turned again to Dan. "I need another six-gun and a rifle. Got them?"

The hotel man bowed his head.

"And I need a horse. I can't go to the livery, of course. Who has one stabled close?"

"Tim Ryan, the blacksmith. His house is right across the alley. His stable backs up to it."

"Good. They'll have searched that by now. Can you go over and throw a saddle on?"

"I'll go," said Jenny. "They're less apt to stop me than Dan. Get out of here while I put on some clothes."

Reynolds started to protest that they would be suspicious of Jenny, they having found her in bed. Surprisingly Belle Carstairs spoke.

"I'll go with her. I can't saddle the animal, but I've a notion that none of the TC would stop me."

Reynolds gave her a thin smile, then with Hay he turned

75

out of the room. The hotel man continued on down the stairs, coming back in a few minutes carrying a Spencer rifle and a worn holster from which hung a heavy Navy Colt and a full cartridge belt.

"I've wondered why I kept them." His face was expressionless as he passed them to Boyd. "Now I know."

Reynolds said, "I won't try to thank you."

Hay's voice was as expressionless as his face. "Don't. This may be a decent town to live in again if you get rid of Laws. It's been a little hard to stomach these past couple of years."

Reynolds fastened the belt around his hips, fitting the holster against his leg. He tested the rifle's action and found it good. The girls appeared from their rooms and without a word moved down the rear stairs to the dark kitchen. Boyd went along the hall to his room, gathering up his bed roll, strapping it tightly. He stood for a moment to collect himself, then stepped again into the upper hall and back to the rear window.

Standing to one side so that he could not be seen from below, he studied the alley, watching for movement. He saw none, but he had no doubt that Cleaver's men were down there, waiting.

Then a shadow shifted in the alley and he knew that the two girls were returning from Ryan's stable. He did not move. He waited for two things. He wanted them back inside the hotel, safe, and he wanted to make certain that no TC man had detected them and investigated the stable.

He heard their steps on the rear stairs and went to the door as they came into the upper hall. The English girl was shaking with tense excitement, but Jenny appeared as cool and collected as if she met such situations daily, and he knew a sudden rush of admiration for her.

"The horse is ready. He's tied with a jerk knot. All you have to do is pull the end of the tether if you're in a hurry." A faint smile touched her lips and then was gone. "We did not see anyone, but you'd better wait awhile. The longer you wait the less watchful they'll be."

"I mean to."

"I'll get you something to eat; something to take with

you." She did not wait for his assent, but retreated down the dark stairs.

Belle Carstairs said anxiously, "What do you plan to do?"

He looked at her. She had as much stake in his actions as anyone in the valley, but at the moment he trusted no one fully. There was too much pressure here. Jud Laws was a clever man. Boyd did not for an instant discount the cleverness, and the power was all with him. At the moment Belle Carstairs was not on Laws' side, but if an unforeseen chance came to salvage the TC fortunes, what would her reaction be?

"The best I can," he said. "We'll do everything we can think of to keep Laws from driving that herd out of the valley. But we haven't enough men to stop him outright. We'll have to use whatever tricks are possible. You go and see Bolger Roberts in the morning. Have him with you when you fire Laws."

Her back was straight, her head up as she extended her slim hand. "Good luck. I may be making a mistake. I never met anyone quite like you before."

His mouth quirked. "Which makes us even. I never met anyone like you either."

He saw the warm color come up into her cheeks. He held her hand a moment longer than necessary, and the thought crossed his mind: her family owned the TC; if he won this fight, if he beat Jud Laws and came into control of the valley—what then?

He squeezed the hand and felt the answering pressure, then she pulled away from him and went quickly along the hall to her door. He stood for a moment, looking after her, then hefted his bed roll and descended the stairs to the kitchen.

Jenny was making sandwiches at the worn work-table. She turned as she heard his steps.

"Don't come into the light. I've got the curtains pulled but they might see you through one of the cracks."

He sat down on the steps. He could see her from where he sat and yet not be visible from the windows.

"That's enough food for an army."

"Lord knows when you'll find any more. Do you want some coffee and something now?"

"I guess I do." He was suddenly hungry. He had not been aware of it before.

She brought him a sandwich and a cup. "I'm going to take a look at the yard. If I put my hand to my hair, go back upstairs."

She went to the rear door and opened it, standing motionless, gazing into the darkness. Then she turned back, closing the door.

"Everything seems quiet. Father's in the lobby, watching the front."

She blew out the kitchen lamp, came over and settled herself on the step below him, pulling her legs up under the folds of her skirt. Light drifted down through the open hall door above and faintly showed him her upturned face. They sat so in silence for minutes.

"What do you think of Belle Carstairs?" she asked.

"How do you mean, what do I think of her?"

"She's prettier than Ellen Petrie."

He was startled. "What made you think of that?"

"I don't know. It just popped into my head. She is, isn't she?"

"I suppose so."

"And she's a lady."

"Acts like one."

"And yet she went across the alley with me tonight and helped me saddle that horse. She was scared to death, but she went."

"Weren't you scared?"

"I guess it's what you're used to." Her voice had a studying note. "She's different. She isn't used to people wearing guns and getting killed. She said that never in her life has she heard as many guns as she heard tonight. It made her kind of sick. She said she was tempted to go home and forget the whole thing, only TC is about all her family has left, and with her father sick she doesn't know where to turn."

"You chatter," he said.

"I always do." She was not angered by his words. "Father says I sound like a lonesome magpie."

"You're a funny kid."

"I'm not a kid any more."

"That," Boyd told her, "is a matter of opinion." He stood up, carrying the empty plate and cup with him. He stepped down beside her, bent and kissed her lightly on the forehead. "You'll do to take along." He did not see her flush in the poor light.

"Now you go tell your father to lock the front door and put out the lights. Then both of you go up to bed."

She came to her feet. "And you?"

"I want the place quiet before I leave. All right?"

"All right," She waited for a long minute, then she said softly, "Take care of yourself, Boyd."

She was gone then, out through the dining room door. He heard her talking to her father. Some time later the light went out and they climbed the stairs.

CHAPTER NINE

HE SAT for another hour on the steps, listening. Finally, he slipped into the darkened lobby and took a careful look at the street. Two men were standing at the corner; he had no doubt that the full length of the alley was covered. He had no watch, but the feel of dawn was in the air. He went back to the kitchen. He could not wait much longer.

He lifted his bed roll and reached for the back door, stopping to examine the yard before he stepped into its shadows. Somewhere a rooster crowed, although there was still no light in the eastern sky.

He crossed to the gate, opening it quietly and again peering out before he ventured beyond it. The narrow alley was in deep shadow, masked by the row of buildings that cut off the low-hanging moon. Two jumps took him across it, and there he crouched beside the wall of the blacksmith's barn, holding the rifle ready, waiting tensely for the cry that would announce he had been seen. None came.

He eased the door open and slid inside. A horse shifted uneasily in the darkness. He fumbled along the stall wall and found the animal. It tried to crowd him and he shoved it over with his shoulder, finding the rope, jerking its end loose and freeing it from the bridle. He backed it out of the stall and, still in the barn, swung up into the saddle.

He had to duck his head to ride out of the door. In the alley he turned not north, but south, heading directly for the jail. He reached the side street without incident, abruptly raking the horse's flanks with his heels. The startled animal leaped forward, crossing the thoroughfare in three wild lopes.

A cry rang from the corner of the main street on Boyd's left. A gun broke the stillness of the night with its quick bark. Then he was again in the alley, charging down it toward the courthouse.

Three men dashed around the building into his path. He fired twice, seeing one drop. The others he rode down, glimpsing their shocked faces as he raced past.

He crouched low, swinging around the corner of the jail, diving across the sandy square which flanked the courthouse. Shots spattered at him from the steps of the building. Other shots came from the corner below. He heard the angry whisper of bullets above and around him, but miraculously he went unhit.

And suddenly he was beyond the last straggling buildings of the town, and free.

He knew that behind him men were running for horses, that within three minutes they would be in pursuit, for Max Cleaver and Jud Laws had put a price upon his head.

But he had already gauged the horse he rode. It was long-barreled and deep-chested, built for endurance and speed, and it wanted to run.

He eased it somewhat. He was still heading south, and he guessed that they would expect him to turn north soon, toward the Crossing. They would try to cut him off from that direction.

But this was a game he understood better than the men

who would follow. He angled west, toward the hills, crossed one creek and then a second. Once in the highlands he had little fear of being found, for he knew every foot of that rugged ground.

Daylight came as he approached the valley's edge. He turned up a brush-grown draw. It would lead him over the military ridge rising ahead, then drop him into a twisting valley which ran northwest. At the head of this he would pick up a little-used trail swinging back toward the Crossing, coming again into the valley just north of the old Running R buildings.

He took his time, conserving his horse's strength. He would have to send the blacksmith some money when he got any. He wondered idly if Alf Bentley had any, and grinned grimly at the thought.

He was now the legal manager of the TC. He had a crew of hill men at his back. And there was probably not five dollars among them all. No one had ever gone into battle with less.

At noon he paused beside a small spring and ate two of the sandwiches Jenny had made. Then he rode on. It was full dark when he dropped into the valley and saw the lights in his old home glow in the far distance. Apparently Jud Laws still had a crew at what was now his northern line camp.

He knew an impulse to ride toward it, to throw half a dozen shots into the buildings, but this he crowded down. Instead, he turned north again, staying away from the river, fearful that a trap might have been set along the main trail.

It was near midnight when he swung into the mouth of the canyon, and he had progressed less than half a mile up this when the challenge came.

"Hold up. Who are you?"

He looked at the dark slope above him, but the moon was not strong enough to let him pick out the sentinel. It might, of course, be one of Laws' men, but he doubted that. Alf Bentley would not have permitted the TC to come into this canyon now.

"Boyd. Boyd Reynolds," he called. "Is Alf up there?"

81

There was a momentary silence, then the voice answered. "He's at the Crossing. You got company?"

"Haven't seen anyone all day."

"Good. Ride in."

He rode on, and as he approached the burned town a man stepped from the charred ruins of the hotel, a rifle at the ready. Plainly Bentley's crew was jumpy.

"Hold it." The man sounded nervous.

"It's Reynolds."

High, jittery laughter came back. "We thought you was dead, likely."

"I take a lot of killing," Boyd told him drily. "Where's Alf?"

"Up at the Dorn mine shack. We're bunking there."

Reynolds rode on up the canyon. Bentley's men had converted the old mining office into a sleeping room. It was one of the few buildings in camp that had escaped the fire. He left his horse and pushed open the sagging door, and heard a curse within.

"Who's that?"

"Reynolds."

There was silence, then a match made a scratching sound. The little flame leaped to life and a man at the far end lit a battered lantern. In its glow Boyd saw the men stretched across the rough floorboards in an ordered row.

They sat up raggedly, huddling in their blankets, heavy with unfinished sleep. Alf Bentley struggled to his elbow.

"So you made it."

Reynolds did not trouble to answer this. "How many men did we lose?"

Bentley fell to cursing. "Two. One at the jail, one at the north end of town. They were laying for us."

"I know it. They shot at me as soon as I dropped out of the window."

"Who told them? Roberts?"

"I doubt it. More likely they saw him ride out and trailed him." He looked around the room, counting the men. There were only eight present.

"Where are the others?"

"Mack and Pete are on guard."

"But there were more."

Bentley cursed again. "We lost two in Kernville; the others had enough. They went over the hill."

Bentley felt a wave of depression. He had counted on more help. Even counting the men who had defected, the odds were much in favor of Jud Laws and his fighting crew.

Still he had one advantage, Laws was trying to get the cattle out of the valley. His job was to keep the man from succeeding.

He said as much now. "From this moment, you boys are riding for the TC."

Each of them reacted to these words. Slim Maynard exploded. "What kind of hocus-pocus is this?"

"We've just been made legal." Boyd laughed, deeply, without sound. He explained his interviews with Belle Carstairs. "She's being robbed the same way we are, so she's on our side. I'm her new manager, and you are riding for me. When this is all over, if there's any question, we were in the right as far as legality goes. Jud and Max Cleaver are in the wrong."

Alf Bentley said dryly, "That won't keep Cleaver from hanging any of us if he gets the chance."

"It won't. Whatever we do, we do ourselves. And some of us will probably be killed. If you want out, now is the time to saddle up and ride away."

Not a man moved.

"I can't promise you much reward. I can get my ranch back if we win. All I need is a fair hearing in the courts. I don't know about the rest of you."

Alf Bentley spoke again for the grouped men. "Most of us want a good crack at Jud Laws. What comes after that, we'll wait and see."

Reynolds nodded. "They've got thirty men at least. We have eleven. But they have to gather cattle and hold them. Most of Laws' crew is going to be too busy chasing cows to fight much. Our chance lies in making it as hard for them as we can. And if we kill anyone in the process, remember, they are stealing TC stock.

"Now, we've got one job to do together, then I'm splitting us into three bunches. Alf will lead one. Slim Maynard will take the second and I the third. The point is to stay in the hills, never give them an open fight. But whenever they get a gather together, scatter them before they can be driven out.

"First, I need two hours' sleep."

He dumped his bed roll on the floor, unrolled it and wound himself in the single blanket. Three hours later he was again in the saddle, riding down the canyon with ten men at his back.

"Our first aim is the old Running R. Cleaver won't have left too many men there. He'll need every rider available if he's going to comb the range. They won't be at the line camp, and we need supplies."

Alf Bentley laughed. "I like this. TC buying our grub."

"You're forgetting," Reynolds told him, "we are the TC crew. As of this morning, any of Cleaver's men who touches a TC cow is rustling. Can't you understand that?"

It brought the first laughter he had heard from these men, and that was good. Men fought better when they could laugh.

"Now let's go get our line camp."

The sun was just breaking across the eastern hills when they rode into the yard. A trickle of smoke, light as a yellow feather, trailed from the cookshack, bringing a pang of memory to Boyd Reynolds. Then he saw the cook come to the door, yawning, having heard the horses.

The yawn died and he stared at the intruders with eyes which threatened to bug from his head.

"What the—?"

He never finished the sentence, for he was looking into the barrel of Boyd Reynolds' rifle.

"How many men are here?"

The cook gulped. "Three besides me. They're still asleep."

"In the bunkhouse?"

The cook nodded, unable to find further words.

"Watch him." Reynolds swung the horse across the yard toward the long, low log building. Half the crew followed him. The rest stayed beside the cookshack.

Reynolds swung down. Most of his youth had been spent in this building, for when he was growing up he had loved to bunk with the crew. He threw his reins to Slim Maynard, pulled Dan Hay's revolver, and picked the door open.

There was enough morning light to show him the tiers of bunks, six on each side of the room. Someone stirred and sat up in the lower one, nearest the door.

"Hey—"

Reynolds' voice was tight. "On your feet. All of you."

They scrambled out, their long hair tousled, their eyes blurred with sleep. The long underwear in which they had gone to bed made them look like three red bears.

"Who in hell are you?" The man in front was short, wiry, with a thin head and close-set eyes. Reynolds had never seen him before.

"Boyd Reynolds. The new TC manager."

"The hell you are. You're the one they threw in jail. I saw you—"

"Never mind." Boyd moved the gun suggestively. "Outside, all of you."

"Now wait—"

"Move, I said." He backed through the door, keeping them covered.

Slowly, unwillingly they followed him out, shivering in the morning chill.

"Slim, go in and get their guns, then throw out their duffle."

There was a wicked look of immense satisfaction on Maynard's face as he stepped from the horse and disappeared into the bunkhouse. A stream of boots, pants, shirts, coats came sailing through the door to land in the dust. The mounted men watched impassively, but there was the glint of pleasure in their eyes. Not one of them but had suffered at the hands of these TC men. And every one of Cleaver's crew were gunfighters, arrogant and cruel, who enjoyed lording it over their victims.

"Get dressed."

Slim Maynard said, "All but their boots."

Reynolds looked toward the doorway. Maynard's face was set and he met Reynolds' eyes with a challenge. "They made me walk away from my ranch without boots. It took weeks for my feet to heal."

"All right," said Reynolds. "No boots." His eyes narrowed reflectively on the three men. One of them might well have killed Hugh Reynolds.

The short man began a protest. "Wait until Cleaver hears about this—"

"He isn't going to hear it from you. Shut up while you still have your pants, or do you want to walk out without them?"

"What—? Walk out?"

"You're to be herded as far as the Crossing and out on the hill trail. You can't miss it. But if you try to circle back, you'll be killed. It's your choice. Slim, get enough food from the cook for three days for them, and take along some breakfast for your people."

"Three days—barefooted? The man was incredulous. "It's seventy or eighty miles across those mountains. We can't make it in three days."

"Then you'll go hungry." Reynolds was unyielding. "Get dressed."

They turned to dressing, sorting out their scattered clothes, muttering to each other but not looking around at their captors. By the time they had finished, Maynard returned, carrying a gunny sack of food across his horse, before the saddle. He dumped it unceremoniously to the ground at their feet.

Reynolds said, "All right, Slim. Take three men and march them up to the Crossing and start them up the trail." He looked down at the prisoners. "If I see any of you again I'll hang you or shoot you on sight."

They lifted their shoulders sullenly. The short man stooped slowly and caught up the sack of food. He hesitated for a moment, then turned and plodded out toward the trail. His partners trooped out behind him and Maynard chose his crew, then looked at Reynolds for final instructions.

"When you've got rid of them, come back here. I'll either leave a message for you or have someone here." He stood for a moment longer before turning to the others. "Let's go see what Cookie has for breakfast."

He led the way to the cookshack. The cook was tall and

thin, as if the food which he had prepared through the years had never agreed with him.

He glared at his new boarders, but made no comment as he filled the plates and set them on the long table.

Sitting down, Reynolds said, "Get together all the supplies there are." He watched the man obey as he ate his breakfast. He ate without relish, hardly conscious of what was before him, his mind planning what had to be done, dividing the valley into sections, estimating the most likely places for Jud to be gathering the cattle.

He finished and motioned Mack to come with him; the two walked up toward the main log building that had once been his home.

He was appalled at the interior of the house. The furniture that had been his mother's pride was torn and battered. The slab table at which they had eaten was scarred by spur marks. He ignored the havoc, shutting his mind to it. He found two cases of rifle shells and one of forty-fives. He and Mack carried them back to the cookshack and distributed the ammunition among the group. Then he had the gathered supplies divided into three parcels. Finally he turned to the cook.

"Clean up this mess, and clean it well. Get your horse, ride into town and draw your pay; then clear out of the valley. I don't want to see you again."

Alf Bentley grunted. "He'll tell Laws what we've done; where we are."

"I want Laws to know exactly what we've done. As to where we are, we won't be here when any of his men arrive. We'll be a long way away."

CHAPTER TEN

JUDGE HERMAN DIXON had for years been a rather unsuccessful attorney. Had it not been for the business thrown his way by the Petrie bank, he might long ago have closed up shop.

He was a man very conscious of his own weaknesses, and very grateful to his benefactors. No one had been more surprised than himself when, two years earlier, Jud Laws had informed him that he was going to run for county judge.

He was not popular, and he knew that, but with Laws' backing he had been elected by a comfortable majority. Since that time he had been called upon to render a number of decisions, all of which had been in favor of the TC ranch.

He had never been paid anything for these decisions, and indeed would have been insulted if any money had been offered. But he was as much a captive justice as if he had been on the TC payroll.

He was a small man with a rolypoly body and thin white hair, carefully parted in the center of his pink head.

He stared over his glasses now, disapprovingly, as Bolger Roberts rose and approached the wooden rail separating the bench from the dusty courtroom.

"What is it now?" His voice was querulous, as though he resented anyone daring to approach him.

Bolger Roberts was sober. He had been entirely sober ever since his return from the Crossing. His hands shook somewhat, and he had difficulty steadying the sheaf of papers he held, but his voice was controlled and his words were spoken plainly.

"I have two actions to bring before this court. One is a restraining order, brought by Miss Belle Carstairs, of London, England, against Jud Laws."

There were only a dozen spectators in the big room, but they began to buzz like so many angry flies. Herman Dixon rapped for order impatiently, peering over his steel-rimmed glasses at the offenders.

"Quiet." He was as upset as they were, but he was careful to hide his feelings. "I do not understand, Counsel."

"It's simple," said Bolger Roberts. "Miss Carstairs, representing the owners of the TC ranch, discharged Jud Laws from his post as manager this morning. She requests an order compelling Jud Laws to vacate all property controlled by the ranch, freezing all bank accounts on which, as manager, he had a power to draw, and restraining him from interfering with her or her duly appointed representatives in conducting the affairs of the ranch company."

Dixon was trying to think clearly and rapidly. He wished that he had had some warning. He cursed Laws for not being there, for not telling him that there was trouble. He cleared his throat to gain a little time.

"This action comes as a surprise."

"Does it?" Roberts' tone was ironic. "At any rate, Your Honor, Jud is no longer manager of the TC, and we want this restraining order."

"And the other action?" The judge bent his head and whispered to his clerk, "Find Jud."

The man rose and scurried through the rear door. Bolger Roberts guessed his errand, but there was no way he could halt it.

"The other is an action brought by Boyd Reynolds to set aside the foreclosure proceedings under which the Kernville National Bank acquired the property known as the Running R. The complaint charges fraud and collusion against Leonard Petrie and Jud Laws, in that they did conspire to deprive the plaintiff of his lawful property."

Again the excited buzz broke out. This time Dixon made no effort to stop it. At least it gave him a few minutes to consider. Then there was an interruption at the rear of the room as Jud Laws appeared. He came down the aisle hurriedly, arrogantly pushing Bolger Roberts out of his way.

"What's going on here?" he asked the judge.

Dixon told him.

Laws swung on Roberts. "What kind of trick is this? I haven't been fired and you know it."

The lawyer gaped at him. "I was with Miss Carstairs when she told you. There were other witnesses."

"Where is she now?"

Roberts could not believe the man's audacity. He stumbled, "Why, at the hotel, I suppose . . ."

Laws swung back to the judge. "Don't you see, Your Honor? This is nothing but a trick cooked up by this drunken sot and Reynolds to cause the TC trouble. You know the sale of the Running R was legal. The case was heard before this court."

Roberts broke in. "You can't get away with this, Jud. There is law in this state even if there is none in this county. Sooner or later it will catch up with you. And when it does, the judge here will also have to answer for his actions."

Judge Dixon's face went red and then white. "Are you daring to impugn this court? I find you in contempt, sir. Sheriff, take him into custody. Put him in a cell and hold him until I am ready to sentence him."

Dodsworth had been an interested observer to the scene. He rose, expressionless, and took hold of Roberts' arm. The old lawyer offered no resistance, knowing that resistance was futile. The sheriff lifted the file of papers from Roberts' hand and passed them across to Jud Laws.

Contemptuously Laws tore them across twice, then dropped them into the clerk's basket. "They're filed," he said, and watched as Dodsworth led his prisoner from the room.

Dixon leaned forward. "I want to see you in my chambers, Jud." He spoke with more authority than he usually used in addressing this man.

Judd looked at him darkly as he followed into the dusty office, closing the door behind him. Dixon turned on him immediately.

"This can't go on." His voice rose as he talked, almost cracking with his indignation. "You've gone too far. That English girl coming here and throwing in with Reynolds has upset everything."

"Why?" Jud Laws' mouth twisted into an ugly line.

90

"Why? Don't be a fool, Jud. If she can't get a hearing here she'll go to the governor. He can send another judge into the county. He can have me removed. He can—" The old barrister ran out of words and spread his hands helplessly.

"That will all take time."

"Yes. But it will happen."

"Let it. I'll take care of it."

"You'll take care of me? How do you intend to do that?" Jud Laws' eyes almost closed. "You're asking a lot of questions all of a sudden."

Dixon wet his lips. "It's not that I don't trust you, Jud —but with Reynolds getting away, that foreclosure on the Running R won't stand up."

"What do I care?" Laws was impatient. "Let the Carstairs woman worry about it."

Dixon wanted more reassurance, but Laws turned on his heel and walked out. He went hurriedly in search of Max Cleaver, finding him as the man came through the batwing doors of the Paradise saloon. Cleaver was laughing heavily, for one door had slammed back against Old Tate as the swamper swept the sidewalk.

Laws was too angry to enjoy the joke. "That doddering old fool Dixon," he said. "We can't hold him in line much longer. He's getting scared."

Cleaver quit laughing. "Oh? What about?"

Laws told him quickly what had happened in the courtroom. "I just told him I hadn't been fired. He threw Roberts in jail, but we've got to silence that English girl. We'll take her up in the hills and hold her until we've run every cow out of the valley."

Cleaver grunted unhappily. "I don't like that. You go messing around women and you will have trouble. If the news gets out across the state that you're holding this one—"

"You got a better idea? Time's short."

Cleaver had no better idea.

Jud Laws waited for his admission, then laughed shortly. "So. Bring a few of the boys to the hotel. We'll take her up to the camp at Black Hawk. When we're finished, she

91

can have the TC and she and Reynolds can fight about who owns the valley. There won't be a cow to split between them."

Jenny Hay and Belle Carstairs were together in the hotel dining room when Jud Laws strode in. He wasted no time on preliminaries.

"Get your things," he directed Belle. "We're taking a ride up into the hills for a few days."

She was caught completely by surprise. "Indeed? And why are we doing that? In view of our conversation this morning I no longer feel that you have anything to say about me or the TC."

"Never mind that. You're in danger here. I'm taking you away for your own safety's sake."

"I'm afraid you're mistaken, Mr. Laws. I'm going nowhere with you."

Jud Laws' voice was as cold as ice. "You're going, one way or another, if I have to rope you on a horse. Act nice and you won't get hurt. Try anything fancy and I have no idea what will happen."

Jenny Hay felt a sharp foreboding that Laws had at last cast aside his mask. She said now, "You've lost your mind, Jud. Even Dodsworth won't sit still and let you kidnap a woman."

He turned on her. "You think he can stop me?"

She had a sickening certainty that no one could stop him, that he had the force, the power to do anything he chose in Kernville, and that the men who rode for him would obey any order without question.

"Don't do it," she said. "If you do, I'll get word to the governor. I'll—"

Feet tramped across the lobby and Max Cleaver came in, followed by three riders. Laws was gaping at Jenny, and she could have bitten out her tongue for her outburst as he laughed.

"So you want trouble, too? I'll give you some. Get your stuff. You're going along."

"Who's going where?" Dan Hay appeared in the kitchen doorway. "What are you doing in my hotel?"

Laws did not even look at him. "Keep out of this, Hay. Your daughter and Miss Carstairs are going up into the hills for a few days. If they behave themselves, they'll come back all right."

"Damn you." Dan Hay's hands tightened into fists at his sides. "If I had a gun—"

Jud Laws' whole morning had been a series of frustrations. His temper, usually kept under careful control, flared. He took two steps and hit Hay in the mouth, knocking the hotel man back through the doorway.

Hay stumbled, trying to catch his balance. Blood leaked from a cut across his lip. He came up hard against the meat block. A long knife lay there. His fingers closed around the handle, and blindly he charged at Laws.

Laws shot him through the body. Jenny froze for a moment, then ran forward and dropped beside her father, cradling his head against her breasts, not realizing he was dead.

She was like a sleepwalker when they lifted her to her feet, in a wordless shock, without reaction of any kind. Bell Carstairs stood, just as stunned. Even Cleaver was shocked.

"Did you have to do that?"

Laws swore at him. "Send two boys to bury Hay, then get some horses into the alley and haul these women out of town."

A small crowd was gathering in front of the building as Laws came out, and Dodsworth came hurrying up, attracted by the shot.

"What happened?"

"Dan Hay went for me with a knife."

The sheriff looked unhappy. "Now wait a minute, Jud. In town—"

"I've got four witnesses." Laws was raging inside, but his face was an icy mask. "You want me to call them before the judge?"

Dodsworth hesitated.

"Don't waste my time," Jud said. "I'll give Dixon a statement. If you want more later you can have it. Hay was drunk."

He turned angrily toward the courthouse and after a moment Dodsworth followed.

Herman Dixon watched in resignation as they came in, and winced when Laws made his short speech.

"Jud. No. Not Dan Hay."

"I tell you he was drunk," Laws said flatly. "Max and Tobe and Ernie and Tupper were all there. They saw it. They'll testify."

Dixon knew they would. A constriction bound him, as though he were being crushed in the coils of a huge boa constrictor. He wished he had never seen Jud Laws. He wished he had never been elected judge. But a look at the man's eyes told him there was no escape for him. It was justifiable homicide as far as the record would go. Anything Jud Laws wanted was justified.

He watched them leave the courtroom, then used the back door and hurried along the alley to the bank. The place was empty when he entered, and he said to Mark Austin behind his window, "Len busy?"

Austin shook his head and Dixon went on to the private office.

Leonard Petrie looked up in surprise. "Why, Judge, don't tell me you want to borrow some money?" It was his attempt at a joke.

Dixon did not smile. "I thought you ought to know." His tone was grim. "I think Jud Laws has finally gone crazy."

The baker was at once concerned. "What do you mean?"

"He killed Dan Hay."

Petrie came out of his seat like a shot.

"He says Hay came at him with a knife, that Hay was drunk. That last isn't true. I know. I'm guessing here, but I think he plans to take that English girl someplace out of his way. He's moving out of the valley, Len, lock, stock and barrel. He's taking all the cattle with him."

They looked at each other in strained silence—two old men who knew they were captives, that they were not strong enough to make a stand. Petrie's voice came painfully.

"What happens then?"

"God knows." The judge used his handkerchief to mop

his forehead. "The man's an egomaniac. He thinks he is God, because he has thirty guns behind him."

Petrie sat down slowly. "He's got that ranch in Wyoming. He's got friends up there. Once that herd is across the line the TC people can whistle for their cows. By the time they can bring suit in the courts up there, the herd will be split and sold."

"And what becomes of us?"

Petrie spread his hands. "Without cows this country will be dead. Without the TC, Kernville might as well pack up and move away."

"And that's not all," Dixon sounded like doom itself. "I've got Bolger Roberts in jail, but he isn't going to stay there. And when he gets out he's going to file suit against you and the bank on the foreclosure of the Running R. I never asked you before. Did Hugh Reynolds actually sign that mortgage, or was it a forgery presented after his death?"

Leonard Petrie went white. Dixon shrugged. "Don't answer. But just remember, Boyd Reynolds is still around. If he lives, a day of reckoning is coming, and I don't trust Laws to protect us."

He left then, and Petrie sat rigidly at his desk. He was still sitting there half an hour later when his daughter came into the office.

She was talking almost before she had closed the door. "Father, there are all kinds of stories flying around town. They say Jud killed Dan Hay and kidnaped both Jenny and the English girl—"

He lifted his eyes to stare at her, and she read the stark fear in their depths.

"Father—what's the matter? Has the whole world gone mad?"

"I guess it has." He could hardly speak. "At least it's coming down around us. Jud's running out."

She showed her disbelief. "Running—how?"

"Taking all the cattle out of the valley. Stealing them, would put it better."

"He's lost his mind."

Her father nodded slowly. "He's making the mistake a

95

lot of men have made before him. They became so powerful that they came to believe nothing could stand against
them. But you can go so far in this country, then it will
rise up. Jud has passed his point. When he killed Dan Hay
and kidnaped those girls he signed his death warrant. Someone will get him. Maybe Boyd Reynolds. I'd say, good
riddance, except that Boyd will bring us down along with
Jud."

She watched him narrowly. "Maybe I can talk to Boyd."
She saw the faint light of hope grow in his eyes and felt
a little disdain. Ellen Petrie had never had any illusions
about anyone. She wanted much from life, and she had
been prepared to get it in the only way open to her.

She left the bank and moved along the street toward
Learner's store. As she passed the blacksmith shop, Jud
Laws came around the corner, and for a long moment they
confronted each other in uneasy silence, then she said
acidly: "Jud, what's this I hear you are trying to do to us?"

Jud Laws read the stern disapproval in her face. For as
long as he could remember he had wanted this girl. As he
grew up he had watched her dancing with other men, prin-
cipally Reynolds, never glancing in his direction, never
giving a sign that she knew he existed. More than anyone
or anything she had shaped and molded the course of his
ways. It had been his determination to win her that had
started him on his grab for power, for he correctly read her
desires.

And now, to meet her open challenge of his tactics, cut
through him as nothing else could have.

In bewilderment he said roughly, "What's the matter
with you? You knew what I was doing. I'm going to be the
biggest man in this end of the country. You were willing.
You and I are cut from the same cloth. What we want, we
take."

Her own anger rose at his bald words. "Yes. I want things.
But I haven't lost my perspective. You had this valley
under control. In another few years we could have taken
over easily. But you had to antagonize this English chit.
You couldn't wait and play carefully."

"She won't stop us."

"What are you going to do, kill her as you killed Dan Hay? You've panicked."

He glared at her, speechless.

"I want no part of your stupidity. I want never to see you again."

She walked past him, her head held very high, acutely conscious that the man behind her did not move.

CHAPTER ELEVEN

FROM HIS LOOKOUT POST on a jutting arm of the foothills which rimmed the western edge of the valley, Boyd Reynolds watched the swirling dust clouds below him. There, he knew, Jud Laws' crew were working their way down the flat lands, driving everything that walked before them.

It was no part of Reynolds' plan to go into open battle against them. He was outnumbered three to one, and Laws' riders were gunfighters first, cowmen second. By comparison, his own people were a weak lot, small ranchers driven from their homes, unsteady and bound to him only by their common hatred of Jud Laws.

If the pressure became great, they would merely fade into the hills, and he would find himself standing alone. With no illusion, he studied the three with him as they loafed in the casual shade of a stunted pine. Nondescript, their clothes patched, their bearded faces gaunt from too many meals missed, their eyes held the vacant shadow of all but abandoned hope.

He caught them regarding him with a vague speculation, as though they had little more confidence in him than he had in them, yet they were all he had.

Alf Bentley and his tiny group were on the far side of the valley, with orders to avoid fighting, yet to disrupt the gathering of the cows in any way they could. Slim Maynard, returned from shoving the three barefoot prisoners up the canyon trail, had now ridden away toward Death Canyon. Their orders, too, were to stay out of trouble, to do nothing unless the drive reached the pass, then to ride for whatever reinforcements Reynolds had remaining.

Night came slowly, filling the valley with the first shadows. The four ate a cold supper, not risking a fire, then Boyd gave his order to mount and led them down the narrow draw, out onto the open floor.

A good three miles ahead of them they caught the wink of the supper fires as the roundup crew settled down for the night.

Clouds ran across the sky in a dark wedge, blotting out the fat rising moon, and the wind which had risen with nightfall whipped about them like a chilling ghost.

The group rode in single file, Boyd in front, pacing them at an unhurried gait. He wanted the horses as fresh as possible when they came upon the herd.

The sounds of the dark mass of animals reached them before they saw it, the cows moving restlessly, the bawling of lost calves, the protesting noises of edgy steers, the monotonous singsong of the night riders as they circled endlessly, soothing and quieting the uncertain beasts.

Within the cover of these sounds Reynolds made a wide circuit around the bed ground, to approach the herd on the side farthest from the camp. There he pulled up, motioning his men around him. They came in, shivering under the blast of the wind which pierced their worn coats. They made a pitiful force for this task.

At least, he thought, nature was playing his part. Had the night been still, the clink of their hoofs on the rocks would have carried ahead of them. Had there been a bright moon they could never have come this close undetected.

"I'm going in," he told them in a low voice. "Wait until you hear me shoot, then hit the herd, hard, and keep them moving. I want those cows scattered from here to the Crossing by morning. We'll meet on the hill where we spent the day."

He did not wait for possible argument, but swung his horse away, picking a careful path in the shrouding darkness, sensing rather than seeing the bunched cattle. He had no knowledge of how many were in this gather. He could hear and smell them, but could not see them.

He edged in, guided by the croon of the night rider, listening to the toneless, off-key rhythm as the man made his swinging circle, waiting for him to pass, for the sound to fade.

Then, suddenly, with a wild yell, he drove his horse in, pulling his six-gun, squeezing the trigger so that his shots blended into one continuous burst of noise.

He heard the frantic bellows of the spooked cows and hauled up, reloading his gun. Behind him rose the yells and firing of his three men.

Then the animals were moving, a darker, waving mass in the gloom, its sound swelling.

Without warning, a rider came out of the blackness, driving directly toward him. He could not tell whether it was friend or foe until the other's gun exploded, close to him, then he fired in return. A low, keening cry came back to him, and the shadowy horse reared, swung about and drove in terror straight into the churning herd.

The mass was in confusion now, its panic flaring. The basic suspicion of a steer makes any untoward noise a threat, and his imagination borrows terror from his fellows.

Their movement now was flight. Running, the herd hit the roundup camp, flowing over and scattering fires, men and horses. The night filled with sound, the shrieking of the horses, the men's high cursing, and over it the constant drum of gunfire from Reynolds' men.

Once under way, he knew, these steers would continue running until they hit the rise of the hills, and there the group would break apart, some few seeking refuge in each of the hundreds of small draws that ran like fingers back into the broken land.

He followed into the cloud of black dust, firing and yelling to speed the stampede. Then he was in the center of the wrecked camp. Around him half a dozen fires smoldered, and one blaze had miraculously escaped destruction where the herd had split to race past.

The glow from this spread in a diffused red light, and

into its orbit three mounted men suddenly materialized. For one instant he thought it was his crew, then as a yell ran toward him, he knew his mistake. The man in the lead was Max Cleaver, shouting and pointing his hand. They sat like statues for a second of shock, then Cleaver shouted.

"It's Reynolds! Get him!"

Boyd fired. The man on Cleaver's right threw up his hands and pitched headlong out of the saddle. The third horse reared, spun and bolted into the night. Boyd aimed and fired again, only to hear the sickening click as the hammer of his gun struck on an already exploded shell.

Cleaver was driving on him, firing. One bullet went through Boyd's hat. The second nicked his forearm and drew a shallow crease along the skin. The third killed his horse.

The animal stumbled, plunging forward, and Boyd was thrown over its head. He lit on his shoulder, rolling, and came up barely before Cleaver could ride him down. He leaped aside, and as the horse shot past, he grabbed Cleaver's leg, literally dragging the big man from the saddle.

They crashed down together, missing the fire by inches. Both had lost their guns, and the fall had broken Reynolds' grip. They came up at the same time, facing each other like two wrestlers, crouched, their arms hanging tense, watching each other in the jumping light of the blaze.

Then with an oath Max Cleaver charged. Boyd side-stepped. The man dived past and Boyd hit him heavily on his cheek. Cleaver stumbled to his knees, then came up with a knife in his hand.

The fire glinted from the long blade wickedly, focusing all of Boyd's attention on it. And Cleaver jumped, holding the knife low, its point tipped up, making an upward-cutting thrust, reaching for Boyd's stomach.

Reynolds leaped away and the knife sliced through the thick fabric of his coat. It caught there and was jerked from Cleaver's grasp by Reynolds' spin. It fell to the ground, and both dived for it. Cleaver got the hilt and Boyd the tip of the blade, and as Cleaver rolled, the sharp edge drew down through the thick heel of Boyd's left hand.

Ignoring this, Reynolds dug his heels against the earth

and heaved back, seeing Cleaver's swinging lunge bury the steel deep in the gritty soil.

Cleaver wrenched again and again, trying to free the weapon, then Boyd's injured hand closed upon the wrist, anchoring it. With his free hand he battered Cleaver's face, once and then again, the second blow smashing full against the mouth.

Cleaver spat blood and teeth and curses even as Boyd hit him again. Feeling the grip on the knife hilt relax, Boyd struck once more. Cleaver fell sideways, trying to roll. Boyd bent, catching the knife in his right hand and yanking it free. He spun as Cleaver was coming up, and drove the sharp blade into the man's breast.

Max Cleaver collapsed onto his back. A gurgling sound came from him. He stiffened as if making one last effort to gain his feet, then his body twisted and was quiet, sprawled on its side.

Boyd was on his knees, sobbing for breath. He crawled forward, the knife still held ready, but it was not needed. Max Cleaver was dead.

Boyd Reynolds stayed on his knees for a long interval. The noise of the running herd had long since faded across the valley. His men were gone. Cleaver's men were gone, probably trying to turn the stampede. He was alone in the wreckage of the camp, alone with two dead men and the unquenched fire.

Slowly he rose to his feet, conscious now of the blood that dripped from the fingers of his left hand. He turned it palm up and examined the cut. It was deep, reaching the bone of the little finger, yet when he tried he found that he could move the others slightly. He crossed and tore a strip from Cleaver's shirt, making a tourniquet and fastening it around his upper arm. He felt weak and dizzy, and all his muscles ached.

He turned and searched the ground, locating his gun. He was awkward, loading it with but the one hand, but he got it done and dropped it into his holster. Then he searched for and found Cleaver's weapon, loaded it and tucked it beneath his belt.

Noise made him swing around. A horse was approaching,

nervously, stopping just in the edge of the circle of light, its reins trailing.

He walked toward it slowly. It was spooky, edging away from him uncertainly, but it had been trained to stand when the reins trailed. He spoke to it soothingly, holding his breath. He needed that horse. If he failed to catch it he would be alone, afoot in the hostile valley, and daylight was coming. It would overtake him before he could reach the safety of the hills.

Apparently he had lost a lot of blood. His head swirled foggily and his knees felt as if they were made of water.

The horse had ceased to roll its eyes, but it still side-stepped, keeping just out of his reach. And then he managed to get one foot on the rein. He stooped carefully, nearly losing his balance as his head reeled. But he got hold of the line. The horse danced skittishly, smelling the blood, but now he had control. He slid the rein over the bowed neck, grasped the horn with his good hand, raised his foot to the stirrup, and dragged himself up.

The animal was jittery and he swayed dangerously, afraid that he would fall. But the horse had worked hard that day and was still too tired to follow through with its protest.

There was now no feeling in his hand and it would not obey his mind's commands to move the fingers. He weighed his choices. He needed a doctor, and there was only the one in Kernville. Going to him was a risk he would have to take. The chances were good that all of Jud Laws' gunmen were somewhere on the range, conducting the mammoth drive. The only person he need worry about in town was Sheriff Dodsworth.

He turned the horse toward the town. It was a good forty-mile ride, and he wondered if he could make it. Yet he knew that he must try to keep the weary horse moving.

Half a dozen times the plodding animal stopped, demanding rest, and he let it stand for a few minutes each time, then urged it on.

He was still five miles from his goal when the sun came from behind the sharply molded eastern hills, killing the shadows which had lingered through the cold of the false dawn.

His whole arm now was numb and he was chilled through. He rode, sustained only by grim determination. Far to the east a dust cloud spiraled into the sky, and he judged that this was another of Jud's crews, gathering cattle. He wondered where Alf Bentley was and if Bentley had scored during the night. But at the moment the questions were academic. He was too weary to really care.

The town was hardly astir in the early day when he turned the horse into the baked yard of the doctor's log house. He saw no one as he half lifted, half fell from the saddle. He held onto it for support until he reached the porch, then pulled himself up by the roof post, staggered against the door and pounded on it. Calling the doctor's name, he felt that his voice was too weak to be heard.

He nearly tumbled through the opening as Mrs. Harmon opened the door. She stared at the weaving figure, the bearded, dirt-caked face, the bloody shirt and bound hand.

"Seth! Seth . . !"

Then the doctor was in the doorway. He was long past middle age, but he still stood as straight as he had the night he brought Boyd Reynolds into the world.

"Boyd! Boyd boy!"

Boyd took a step forward, stumbled, then steadied himself, leaning against the jamb. Seth Harmon caught him beneath his arm and supported him inside and to a chair, saying, "Mother, get some coffee."

Mrs. Harmon went with quick, birdlike steps toward the rear of the house, returning almost before Boyd was seated, carrying a steaming cup.

"Son, whatever happened to you?"

Boyd made a poor job of trying to smile. "I had an argument with Max Cleaver."

She shuddered. "There's a horrible man. Someone should do something about him."

"Someone did," said Boyd, and lay back against the chair.

The doctor had turned to a cupboard, found a pint bottle and laced the coffee heavily with whiskey. Boyd noticed that Harmon was still in his undershirt, and it made him want to smile again, but he could not.

"Drink this." Harmon held the cup to his lips and Boyd drank. "Now let's see that hand."

The bandage was stuck with clotted blood. Mrs. Harmon brought warm water, and the cloth was soaked free, the doctor whistling soundlessly when the cut was uncovered. He poured a second drink into the cup and Boyd felt the warmth run through him, as of returning life.

As he drank, the doctor bathed the hand, then sewed the edges of the wound together. Reynolds winced each time the needle pierced his flesh, but the arm continued numb, dulling the actual pain. As her husband bound clean bandages around the hand, the woman brought fresh water and washed Boyd's face.

When both had finished, the doctor said, "There. Now we'll get you into bed."

A protest formed on his lips, but Boyd found that he could not stand, and together the Harmons half carried him into the adjoining room. Five minutes later he was deeply asleep.

He waked, and was unable for minutes to remember where he was. He lay puzzled, staring at the unfamiliar ceiling, then a noise at the door made him turn his head and he saw Mrs. Harmon peer through at him.

"What time is it?" was his first question.

Her smile was quick and warm with relief. "Way past noon."

"I've been asleep all morning?"

"Son, you've slept the clock around, and then some. More than twenty-four hours."

Comprehension came to him slowly, and then jarringly. "I've got to get out of here."

"No. You stay for another day, at least. You lost a lot of blood."

"I can't. Every minute I lie here Jud Laws is moving that herd closer to the pass. But I ought to see the English girl before I leave—could you get word and ask her to come here? It would be safer if I kept off the street."

Mrs. Harmon gave him a strained glance. "Haven't you heard?"

"Heard what?"

104

The words came hard for her. "Jud Laws killed Dan Hay and carried off Belle Carstairs and Jenny."

Boyd Reynolds threw back the covers and swung his feet to the floor. "He what?"

"That's the story. It's all over town. The sheriff has gone out to look for them. He took both his deputies, and he hasn't come back. I think he finally got frightened of being Jud's cat's-paw."

Reynolds was casting about, trying to reshape his plan. If Jud had the girls, he also held the whip hand, for Reynolds would not dare jeopardize their safety.

"Are any of Jud's men in town?" he queried.

"Not a one. He's got them all riding."

"Where are my clothes?"

"The doctor won't like your getting up."

"I can't help it. I have to go. Where are they?"

She hesitated a moment longer, then noting the grim set of his face she hurried off. When she brought the things, he saw they had been cleaned and ironed. He did not try to thank her, for his full mind was on this newest problem.

He dressed hastily, and when he came from the room she had food and coffee on the table. He tried to ignore it, but she said firmly, "Eat. You may not have another chance for a while."

He sat down and gulped the food and she made disapproving clucking noises. "Slow down, boy. You'll be sick—and take care of that hand."

He nodded, continuing to chew.

"You'll be sorry if you don't," she went on. "If you hurt it again it may get stiff, and stay that way."

"I'll try," he said, and rose, heading for the barn.

She went with him, and he needed her help, cinching the saddle he had thrown on the horse he had ridden in. Then he was up, giving her a brief thanks, leading the horse directly toward the bank. Watchful, but seeing no one to challenge him, he marched silently into Petrie's office. The banker's head came up at the sound, then he froze.

"Boyd."

Boyd Reynolds shut the door, his face dark. "Leonard," he said, "when I was a kid I used to think you were a great man. Now I think you're a thief and a willing partner of Jud Laws. But I can't believe you are low enough to be a party to the kidnaping of two women."

Petrie's face drained of all color. He tried twice before he could bring out his words. "I swear I had nothing to do with that."

"Tell me where they are."

"So help me, Boyd, I don't know. If I'd known I would have told Dodsworth."

Reynolds' grin was ironic. "How many TC men are in town?"

"None."

"Who might know where he took the girls?"

Petrie spread his hands. My only guess would be Joe Conners at the Paradise. People are apt to talk in a bar."

Boyd nodded and turned out of the bank without thanking the man. Petrie stared after him with eyes grown suddenly old.

Ellen Petrie was crossing the street as Boyd came from the door. He would have ignored her, but she called his name and quickened her step.

"Boyd, wait—what did you do to your hand?"

"Hurt it," he said, letting his impatience show.

"I wanted to see you," she told him quickly. "Have you heard about Jud and those two girls?"

A new sickness went through him. "Ellen, do you know where he took them?"

"I do not," she flared. "I was furious about it. I'm through with that monster, and I've told him so." Then she spoke in a different, soft and questioning tone. "Boyd, I'm sorry. I made a terrible mistake—"

"A little too late to discover it," he said roughly, and was surprised to realize that it was true. All he had ever felt for her was washed out, entirely gone.

"Boyd, please don't desert me—"

"I'm in a hurry," he said, and brushed past her, moving quickly to the saloon without glancing back.

The long room was ghostly quiet, empty of people except for Old Tate, desultorily washing off the top of the poker table, and Connors, polishing glasses behind the bar.

Connors almost dropped the one in his hand. "Reynolds—you're the last person I expected to see."

Boyd waved this aside, leaning across the bar tensely. "Joe," he said. "You hear a lot from that side of this counter. Have you any idea where Jud Laws is holding Jenny Hay and the TC girl?"

Connors looked concerned. "I wish I did, Boyd, but I truly don't." He set out a bottle and glass. "Have one on me."

Tate shuffled away from the poker table, a gnome of a man, his hair white and thin and wispy on his small head. As he passed Boyd he tugged once at his coattail, then jerked his head in an almost imperceptible gesture toward the front door. He went on then, out to the sidewalk.

Boyd had his drink, then moved after the swamper. He found the man standing beside his horse, engrossed in an inspection of the saddle, a secretive, uncommunicative cast-off of the town.

The old man spoke one low word. "Black Hawk."

"The girls are there?"

Tate nodded.

"How do you know?"

Tate growled his resentment. "That big bum, Cleaver, near knocked me down with the door. Then Jud came up and told him to take them to Black Hawk."

CHAPTER TWELVE

THE BLACK HAWK MINE had never been the producer that the Bentley property at the Crossing had been, but through the years one group and then another had attempted to work it. It was idle at the moment, but it had been occupied within the year and the buildings were in good repair.

It sprawled in a side canyon south of Kernville by a

dozen miles, and no more than ten or twelve miles from Death Canyon. Darkness had come again before Reynolds had ridden half the distance.

He had considered first trying to locate Slim Maynard and his two men, then discarded the idea. He could spend the full night searching for them, and he needed darkness as a cover to approach the mine.

He could not know how many guards Jud would have left there, but hopefully there should not be more than two. The roundup would require as many men as could be spared.

The road was a rutted track winding along the narrow canyon's bottom, and in this depth the darkness was deepened. Reynolds gave the horse its head to pick the way, for it could judge better than he. Though the moon was up, the canyon walls closed it out, and the way was as black as a mine tunnel. He rode without haste, listening acutely, and came finally around a bend, feeling rather than seeing that the canyon widened before him.

The tunnel of the mine was driven into the south wall, two hundred feet up the slope, and the buildings clustered about the opening in a hollow square. Below them the dump was a scar of raw dirt spilling down the hillside.

Reynolds dismounted at the curve and tied his horse to a scrub pine. He drew his gun and moved forward as quietly as he could. Here a dip in the canyon rim let the moonlight spill over, silhouetting the weathered buildings above him in its soft glow. And now he could see to pick his route between the rocks that had rolled down into the trail.

He paused often to listen. The night was as still as death, and seemed as lifeless, until he began to suspect that Tate had been mistaken. Then, suddenly, he found the horses.

There were four of them, stabled in the old machinery shed at the foot of the dump. He heard them stir as he passed the partly open door, and took a minute to look inside. Four horses. That probably meant two guards.

He moved on, debating where the girls might be. One possibility was the main bunkhouse, another the building which had been the office. He wished he knew, and wished he knew where the guards were.

He stood looking at each building carefully, but there

was another problem to be faced first. If he climbed the dump he would be an easy target for anyone watching from the windows or the black tunnel mouth, yet this offered the only path upward. The canyon sides to the right and left of the dump's fan were too steep to climb.

An idea came to him and he turned into the machine shed. He freed two of the horses and drove them outside. Then he picked up a couple of rocks and hit them accurately on the flanks. The animals took off downcanyon, their shoes striking sparks from the rocks over which they ran.

At once there was a yell from above. "Harry, Harry, the horses are loose."

Crouching in the shadowed interior of the shed Boyd could look up the moonlit side of the dump. He was rewarded as two men appeared from the bunkhouse, cursing, sliding and slipping down the loose-dirt slope.

He waited until they had almost reached the bottom, then he took careful aim at the one ahead and squeezed the trigger. The echo of the explosion blended with the man's high, startled shriek, then the figure toppled forward, falling headfirst down the remaining distance to the canyon floor.

His companion, caught in the open halfway up the grade, threw a shot toward where Reynolds hid. The bullet went through the shed door and struck one of the two horses still there. Its neigh sounded like the scream of a wounded panther. It plunged, kicking wildly, its hoofs battering loose the boards at the side of the building. Then the halter rope broke and the animal charged for the door, its flying legs knocking Reynolds aside before he could get a clear shot at the man outside.

By the time he had picked himself up, the guard had dived into a small depression at one side of the dump, and all Reynolds could see of him was a part of one leg.

After a long, tense interval the guard sent an inquiring shot through the doorway, the bullet striking somewhere behind Reynolds. Reynolds waited five minutes more, satisfied that the man was growing more and more uncomfortable in his shallow hole.

Finally he called, "Had enough?"

There was no answer.

"You'll have to come out sooner or later. I can move around in here, you can't."

Still there was no answer.

"Throw your guns out and you can walk away. I don't want you. I want the girls."

"All right." The man straightened up. He tossed his rifle down the dump, and then his six-gun. He himself came sliding down the hill.

Reynolds had never seen him before. He stepped from the doorway. He had no warning. The guard was still stumbling, trying to keep on his feet in the loose dirt.

Reynolds did not see where the holdout gun came from. It was suddenly in the man's hand, snapping a shot that barely went past his shoulder.

Boyd shot him coolly, as deliberately as if he were only a painted target. He watched the man fall, then walked forward, cautiously, to be certain that he was dead. From there he went to examine the first guard.

His hand was bleeding again and he judged that it must have opened when the horse knocked him down. He reloaded his gun before he climbed the dump. He felt sure that there were only the two guards, yet he meant to take no unnecessary risks.

The girls were in the mine office, the door fastened from the outside. He opened it and found them waiting, Belle Carstairs white-faced and shaking, Jenny seemingly unmoved.

"Oh, Boyd Reynolds." Belle Carstairs began to cry. "You'll never know how glad I am to see you. Never." She sank down on a bench, burying her face in her hands.

Boyd looked at her helplessly, then went to put his good hand on her shoulder. "It's all right. The guards are dead."

She straightened, taking his hand in both her own and kissing it. He glanced at Jenny and met her watchful eyes, finding them dark, unreadable.

"Are you all right?"

She nodded, pointing to his bleeding bandage. "That needs attention. She moved to him, lifting his wrist and

110

studying the hand. Then she stooped and tore a long strip from her petticoat. "Here." She began to loosen the old bandage.

He heard her draw her breath at sight of the cut, and her face drained a little, but her fingers never faltered. He glanced at the other girl and saw that her head was turned as if she could not look at the wound.

When the fresh bandage was in place Jenny said without expression, "What do we do now?"

Reynolds had been debating the same question. Now that he had rescued them, what did he do with them? Jud Laws' men still controlled the valley, and even if they could manage to cross it unseen, there was no promise that they would be safe in Kernville.

"Is there food here?"

Jenny nodded. "In the cookshack. They took us over there in the daytime and made us cook for them."

"Did they bother you?"

"They talked a lot of vileness to Belle. They didn't pay much attention to me."

"We'll have to get you out of here." He was thinking rapidly. "I think the best thing is for us all to eat something, then you two take horses and head for the railroad. There are still several hours of darkness left, enough to get you down the valley below Death Canyon. That's where Jud will try to put the cattle over the hills.

"Go to the railhead and wait for me there. But first, Jenny, I guess you'll have to help me. Is there a lantern?"

She found one and lit it and together they went down to the tool house. The remaining horse eyed them warily as they came in.

"I hope they left a shovel."

There were several shovels in the pile of tools in a corner, and beside them Reynolds found an open case of dynamite. He eyed it thoughtfully as he picked up a shovel and turned outside.

Hindered by his injured hand, he needed Jenny's help to drag the two bodies together at the foot of the dump. She did not flinch and his admiration for her grew. He used the shovel to push the loose dirt over the bodies, and only then said to the girl: "Your father—I was very sorry to hear about that."

She was still dry-eyed. "If only he had had a gun."

"I had his gun." Boyd knew a sudden stabbing sense of guilt.

"It wouldn't have mattered," she said, "but knowing him, I just wish he had had one."

They turned and climbed the dump. The English girl was waiting for them in the darkness at the top.

"I couldn't bear to stay inside alone." Her voice was shaky. "I kept trying to think what I would do if you two didn't come back. This horrible country—I don't know how anyone lives here."

Jenny's voice was expressionless. "You can get used to anything. Now let's have breakfast."

They turned to the cookshack. Belle went to the stove and fried meat while Jenny put up two bundles of food. They ate hurriedly, then again went down the dump.

"Miss Carstairs, you take this horse," Reynolds said. "Mine's down the hill a way. Jenny can use him." As he spoke he was loading his pockets with a dozen sticks of dynamite, a length of fuse and some caps.

Jenny watched him narrowly. "What are you going to do without a horse?"

"I spooked two down the canyon. They shouldn't have gone too far."

"And the dynamite?"

He said grimly, "If we can't break up the drive, I'm going to close Death Canyon."

She caught her breath. "Then Jud will have to drive to the railroad."

"If he does, we'll have Miss Carstairs there. The sheriff can seize the herd in her name. Remember, the railroad is in a different county."

She nodded briskly. "Go ahead and close the canyon. You're less likely to be hurt that way."

"Oh, please do." The English girl reached out to catch his good hand in both of hers. "Please do. I couldn't stand it if you were killed trying to help me."

112

"I've no intention of getting killed. Now let's go."

The English girl mounted and Jenny and Reynolds followed on foot, down to where Boyd had tied his horse. As they went he cautioned them. He hated to send them down the valley in the night, alone, but it was the safest way, and Jenny knew the country.

"Stay clear of anything that sounds like cattle," he said. "I don't think they can have pushed them this far yet, but there's no way to be sure."

He stood watching them ride into the shadows, both of them turning for a long, silent last glance back at him before they turned the curve. Then he sat down and waited for first light.

As soon as he could see, he went in search of the horses, finding them together in a little meadow of heavy grass close to the canyon's mouth. He was able to get close enough to use the rope he had brought, dropping it over the head of the near animal. Then he led it back up the trail to the tool house, saddled it, tied his grub sack and a blanket behind the saddle, and swung up.

CHAPTER THIRTEEN

THE CUT called Death Canyon was a thousand feet deep, winding like an incision through the spine of the hills. Years ago the river had sorted out this path, and the floods of each succeeding year had gouged it deeper.

In places it was wide, the rubble-strewn bottom stretching up to three hundred feet between the sheer wall and the stream. At others, particularly at the sharp right-hand curve known as the Elbow, the dry, level ground was less than thirty feet. It was here, in this steep and narrow defile, that Boyd Reynolds intended to plant his shots.

113

In the early morning sunlight he had left the Black Hawk mine and ridden down into the valley. As soon as he had turned the lower bend and had his first view of the stretching land, he had seen the dust cloud, only four miles to his north. He checked his horse, watching it.

There had not been time enough to regather the animals he had scattered at the northern end of the valley, then drive them this far. He could only conclude that Jud Laws had abandoned those cows and had begun his drive with only what he had collected to the east and south of Kernville. But this was small solace.

Boyd wondered what had happened to Bentley and the two men with him. Obviously they had not enjoyed his own success in disrupting the roundup.

It left him no choice. His move must be made at Death Canyon, and he was grateful for the chance discovery of the dynamite, for he and Slim Maynard's quartet would not be enough to stand against Laws' full crew.

He descended to the edge of the foothills, alert to every movement below him. In the crisp air he caught occasional glimpses of the herd, and saw that they were being pushed fast. At the rate they were coming, they should reach Death Canyon's mouth sometime before dark.

He himself reached it at noon, turning up along the stream, his eyes closely examining the rocky walls as he progressed. He was half a mile up the narrow pass when he caught the glint of sun on a rifle barrel.

He pulled his horse quickly into the shelter of the overhang and sent his call echoing up.

"Maynard. Slim Maynard."

There came an answering hail and he thought grimly that they had not been too alert to let him come this far without spotting him. Probably their attention had been on the approaching cloud that surrounded the herd.

He called again. "How do you get up there?"

Maynard's voice reached down to him thinly. "Another mile, there's a side draw you can lead a horse up."

He found the draw, a shallow, twisting path, rock-strewn from forgotten floods. Here he dismounted, looped the rein over his arm, and began to climb. It took the better part of an hour before he topped out on a wide ledge, finding Maynard and four men waiting for him.

The extra man was a surprise, for he had been with Bentley. "Where's Alf?"

The other swore. "We rode into an ambush yesterday. Alf and Jeff got it. I waited for dark and sneaked across here. I didn't know where else to go."

Reynolds considered. There were six men, including himself, enough to scatter the herd after nightfall. But to what purpose? Laws still had them enormously outnumbered. He would only round up the animals again. It was still better to block the canyon with a rockslide which could not be crossed.

Quickly he outlined the plan. They left two men with the horses, to keep watch, the rest working along the ridge, seeking the best point of the Elbow's curve. They found it on the up-canyon side, within the narrow neck. At some former time the cap rock had split downward for a hundred feet, and into this fissure earth had washed, deep enough to support several good-sized trees.

Boyd put Maynard and his remaining two men to digging holes in this earth, and himself continued along the ridge, hoping to find a second location, as insurance. But there was none, and he returned, finding the others just finished.

From his vantage point he had a clear view of the herd plodding toward the canyon mouth. The sharp air seemed to magnify them, so that he could even make out the point riders, although they were at least five miles away.

He set the charges himself, careful to tamp them well. He did not want the holes to "blow out." He wanted the full force of the explosion to lift the split rock face and tumble it into the slot below.

He crimped the caps with his teeth as he had seen the old miners do. He cut the fuses. With six holes spaced some five feet apart, he had not enough fuse to connect them together. He set six fuses and assigned one man to light each.

At his signal the matches flared. At his signal each man ignited a fuse. Then all dived for safety over the jagged crest of the ridge.

Reynolds fell into a depression beside Maynard and they lay, their faces buried against the harsh ground. Then the whole mountain shook as the blasts let go. A cloud of dirt rose high into the air. Small rocks showered down on them, knocking a man on Reynolds' right unconscious. With a grinding roar the face shattered and went sliding in a thousand small avalanches into the river.

Far out across the valley Jud Laws and two men were riding point, turning the herd gradually toward the canyon mouth. The shock wave from the mountain rolled over them with jarring force.

Jud reined in, his head jerking toward the mountain's heights, where the dust cloud boiled up, and he guessed at once what it was. A blinding rage shook him harder than the wave's concussion.

Ever since he could first remember, Boyd Reynolds had bested him, a better rider, a better shot, a better dancer. His hatred of Reynolds ran soul deep, and now he all but wept under its torture.

In his battle for power he had been so close to winning, to crushing all opposition and accomplishing his dream. And then Reynolds had appeared, rising from the dead to block his path. Until Reynolds' return everything had seemed in his hands—the valley, the cattle, and Ellen. It was characteristic that he thought of his goals in that order, although he wanted Ellen Petrie more than he would ever want any other woman. And Ellen was now lost to him. He had known it at that last meeting on the street. He had never deceived himself that she was bound to him by anything except fear and hope of gain to herself.

He turned, looking at the herd. He had no doubt that the canyon was closed to him, and his quick mind ran over the other possibilities. There was only one way left to him. He must drive on to the railroad, sell the cows, take the money and leave the country. For with Max Cleaver's death, even the Wyoming ranch was gone.

He cursed himself for ever putting that into Cleaver's name. It had not occurred to him that the fool would get himself killed. When the rider from the north end had brought the word yesterday of finding Cleaver's body in the wrecked camp, Jud Laws had lost all perspective.

It was Reynolds who had killed Cleaver. It was Reynolds, always Reynolds, who blocked him whichever way he turned. He looked again into the mountains, in his mind's eye seeing the man as a giant standing athwart the pass. His hatred was like a festering boil which must be lanced. Nothing else mattered at the moment beyond his need to come face to face with his Nemesis, to destroy him once and for all time.

He was thankful for one thing. The confounded English woman was safely out of his way at Black Hawk. Were she free, she could cause him trouble in selling the cattle.

He swung his horse over to the rider on his right and gave him the necessary orders to turn the herd and drive on to the railroad and hand them over to the cattle buyer there.

He had twenty men with him, and it would take only six or eight to handle the animals. The trail was straight and nearly level, and it was only thirty odd miles to the cattle pens.

He rode slowly around the moving mass, choosing the men he wanted with him. When he drew them all aside he had ten, the toughest members of his crew.

His orders were calculated. "You all heard that explosion. It's my guess it was Reynolds, blowing down the wall and closing the canyon. I don't know who he has with him, but it can't be too many, and they're still in the hills. I want them. Every one of them. But mostly I want Boyd Reynolds."

They looked at him without feeling. They did not share his fierce urgency. He knew this. These men who rode for him had but a single interest: money. His mouth thinned at the thought.

"I'll pay one hundred dollars for each man of Reynolds' crew that you cut down." He waited a full minute for the effect of this to subside, then raised his voice. "And two thousand to the man who gets Reynolds."

That jarred them, and he added, "If more than one of us gets him, I'll split the money among you."

He saw their hard eyes light up. He noted the twitching of their bearded lips, and realized that he was setting in motion one of the great manhunts. With that prize before them they would comb the hills with the relentless patience of a starving cat.

They rode then, leaving the herd behind them. There were still two hours of daylight, and they covered the five miles to the edge of the rising ground in a little over half an hour.

From their vantage point on the rock shelf Reynolds and his little crew watched them come. Below them, thousands of tons of broken rock choked the throat of the canyon as effectively as a cork thrust into the neck of a bottle.

Behind the new barrier the rushing stream was already building a good-sized lake as its trapped water rose. Reynolds' attention had been on the rising pond, calculating what this could mean to the south end of the valley, wondering why it had never occurred to any of them to dam the canyon and create such a reservoir.

"Company."

He looked around as Slim Maynard spoke softly. Slim was squatting on the high point of the ledge, looking out across the valley, and Reynolds moved up to join him. He heard the uneasy stir of the men around him and knew that they were nervous, wary.

"I make it eleven." Maynard's voice was dry. "And I've a hunch they're looking for blood."

Reynolds studied the distant riders intently, hoping that Jud Laws was among them. His desire to face the man was as strong as Laws' to face him.

Maynard said laconically, "They can trap us here in these hills. There's no way up the north wall, and that water blocks us from going up the canyon."

Reynolds looked at him quickly. "How many other trails are there?"

"The draw you used and the track we followed up from the valley."

"No others?"

"None you can take a horse down."

"Jud will know that."

118

"If they've been using this canyon, yes."

He turned, offering the others the decision. "We can leave the horses here and make it out on foot, or we can try to get down the trail before they reach it, and make a run for it."

They stared back at him and he read their uncertainty. Maynard swore.

"I'm for making a run. We should have waited until dark to fire that blast."

"We didn't." Reynolds' tone was short. There was no gain in considering that now. "If we're going, let's go."

They ran to where the horses pawed restlessly at the scant grass tufts among the rocks and swung to the saddles.

Slim Maynard led the way, the others stringing out in single file, Boyd Reynolds bringing up the rear.

CHAPTER FOURTEEN

THE DRAW down which they hastened twisted and turned, leading them through the last barrier of the hills and opening suddenly onto the level valley floor.

As Slim Maynard emerged from this last curve he hauled up, waiting for the men behind him. In so doing he signed his death warrant. Jud Laws' lusting crew had raced across the distance faster than Reynolds had believed possible.

Arrived and already deployed among the fringe of cottonwoods along the river's course, Laws waited. He held his fire until the full troop was exposed, and when Reynolds moved around the rock shoulder, gave his signal. The eleven guns sent out their stunning blast.

Maynard was knocked down first, and his riderless horse dashed northward up the valley. The two men who had drawn to his side were hit in the same instant and sent sprawling from their saddles, lifeless as straw-filled sacks.

The two behind them spun about, leaping for the safety of the canyon they had just left, and in so doing created a momentary shield, protecting Reynolds from the withering fire.

He pivoted his horse. He could not shoot, for he needed his good hand to control his mount. He saw one man go down even as he gained the shelter. The other jumped his horse across his fallen comrade and clattered up the rocky draw.

Then Boyd was around the bend, driving upward, hearing behind him the howls of Laws' men as they poured from their place of concealment and rushed into the canyon.

He spurred on, glancing back across his shoulder as he rounded each successive bend. The shadows were beginning to gather in the defile's recesses, but there was still an hour of daylight on the hills.

If only it were dark he could leave the horse and head out across the broken slope on foot, but that was not possible while they could see. There was not cover enough to cloak his movements.

He reached the high shelf again, beyond which there was no footing for a horse, and found the animal left by his remaining man, its reins trailing, its rider vanished.

A rattle of stones came from above, and Reynolds had a quick glimpse of the figure scurrying like a chipmunk across the face.

Reynolds threw himself from his saddle, pulled the rifle from the boot, and ran for the rising rock wall. He was hampered by the gun, hampered by having only one useful hand.

He climbed, hunting for toeholds in the bald rock wall. Below him the sound of advancing horses, the shouts of the killers, spurred his efforts.

The man ahead was out of sight, lost somewhere in the jumble of scrubby brush and jagged rocks above. The brush was too thin and widely spaced to offer more than minimum cover at Reynolds' level, but three hundred feet upward from the main ledge was a narrow shelf. He clambered toward the shelf and threw himself over its jutting lip. Even as he wriggled behind a narrow breastwork of fallen rock, twisting to lie flat, facing the drop, the first of Laws' riders shot into view beside the horses below him.

He eased his rifle barrel through the cleft of two rocks, but did not fire. He waited, wanting Laws in his sights for his first bullet.

He had no hope that he could survive against the odds. His only satisfaction would be in taking Laws with him.

But Laws did not appear. Whether by accident or design, his enemy was at the tail of the column as it converged upon the shelf.

They sat their horses, looking up, their eyes prying into every possible shelter. And then Reynolds was given unexpected help.

On his left a rifle exploded, and he knew that the man he thought had escaped had instead stayed to join the fight.

The cluster of riders broke into milling panic, without room to separate, completely exposed. Two went down in the rapid firing, a third and then a fourth as Boyd's rifle joined the battle. Answering bullets spattered the rocks around Reynolds. A flying chip cut his forehead.

And then abruptly the men below had disappeared around the curve. The firing stopped. Peering across his shelter, Boyd counted four men and two horses lying motionless.

He called across the slope but got no answer, his voice echoing back to his own ears. He did not know whether the man had been hit or feared disclosing his position.

It was very quiet in the canyon. Somewhere a bird called against the approaching night. The sun was gone. The hollows were already deep in purple shadow. It was the time of peace that Boyd had always relished in the hills, but there was no peace now. Though the killers were out of sight he knew that they had not gone far, and unless his count was wrong, there were still seven gun-hands left.

He shifted his position and reloaded his rifle. His hand pained with a burning ache, for the shooting had opened the wound and it was again leaking blood.

He could do nothing but wait for night. As though he could see it, he pictured at least one rifle trained on his slope from around the nose of the bend.

They, too, were waiting. But they could better afford

the time. They had the advantage of numbers and they had freedom of movement beyond his sight. With full darkness they would begin climbing the mountainside, climbing above him, cutting him off from his possible retreat through the hills.

The shadows deepened, gathering in the canyon and rising around him, and the night was upon them. There was no moon yet above the eastern rim.

He heard Laws' gunhawks, the cautious scrambling sounds as they began to move up the bank. They were trying to be quiet, but now and again a loose rock rolled, ghostlike, betraying their progress. He could no longer remain where he was, and with his crippled hand he could not hope to climb as fast as they.

He did not go up. He went down. He took his time, feeling his way, confident that if he did make some slight noise it would be covered by those searching for him. He did not know how many were on the slope, how many had remained on the trail. His half formed idea was to try to reach a horse, to attempt to ride down whoever would be in his way, relying on surprise as his only chance.

It took him ten minutes to reach the wide, level shelf. Now he heard voices above him. They were crisscrossing, calling to each other as they closed the net he had left.

He turned toward where the horses should be grazing. In the east the sky was now beginning to lighten, although the moon was still behind the ridge.

And then he saw the dark shape of a man outlined against the sky. He recognized the bulky shape and knew that Jud Laws stood within seven feet of him. He froze.

He was within the deep shadow of the bank, and he was certain that Laws had not yet discovered him. His gun was in his hand and it would be a simple thing to squeeze off the five shots it held. He could hardly miss at the distance. But a shot would bring a full barrage from above. However, if he could get close enough to shove the muzzle against Laws' side he might use him as a hostage to permit his passage down the trail.

He took one tentative step forward, testing with his toe

to be certain there was no stone in his path. He took a second step and then a third. And then Jud, staring up the dark bank, caught a hint of movement.

He let out a high, wild, startled yell. He jumped forward instinctively, his arms shooting out, wrapping around Reynolds as he yelled again.

"I've got him! I've got him!"

As he made his grab, his arm struck Reynolds' gun and spun it out of his hand to thud into the darkness out of sight.

Boyd tried and failed to break away. Handicapped by the painful hand, he was not a match for Laws. The heavy arms around his body had closed with the tightness of a vise, and Boyd felt himself smothering. Again he fought to break the grip.

Above him, Laws' cries were being answered, and men were sliding hurriedly down the bank. In a few seconds he would be a prisoner or dead.

He threw himself backward, hoping that as they fell Laws' arms would loosen. They went down heavily with a force that drove most of the air from Reynolds' body, but Laws still held him in the constricting hug.

He rolled, still trying to thrash free. Rolled over once and again, and then there was nothing beneath him. Wildly he knew that they had gone over the edge.

They fell for an eternity. They struck suddenly in the top of a stunted, twisted pine. They hung for an instant. In that instant Laws' clinging embrace broke, and Boyd was alone, turning over and over in the air, expecting at any moment to dash against the hard rock floor of Death Canyon.

The jar came, shocking, sickening, and then water closed over his head, ice water that felt like burning liquid. He went down, his momentum slowing as he sank, until his shoulder struck the bottom.

Instinct only made him kick out, and he rose again with a new panic at his black, airless prison. Then he broke the surface, gasping for breath but unable to see. He took four wild strokes. The fingers of his injured hand slammed down on rock and in his convulsive reaction his head went under. Only the water stifled his scream.

Then he had fought for a footing and dragged himself trembling from cold and shock up the ragged bank. He lay there all but unconscious, too groggy to understand what had happened. Only gradually did it come to him that he had fallen into the lake so newly created by his blast.

He rolled and got to his knees, feeling over his body for broken bones. He could find none. From far above, excited voices trailed down to him, but their faintness lent him a certain security. No one could climb down from the ledge in the present darkness.

He sought cover between two huge rocks, canted together, and huddled there through the time that the moon illuminated the surface of the water and the shore. The voices argued for a long while, and then came the rattle of moving horses. After that, the night was still again.

At first light he found Jud Laws' body. As they careened off the tree, Laws had fallen in a different direction from Boyd. The man lay twisted and broken halfway up the dam.

Oddly, Laws' revolver had remained in its holster. Reynolds stooped, his every muscle crying out in anguish. He lifted the gun and checked it, hope rising in him as he touched the smooth plates of the stock.

He looked up, studying the canyon walls, and could find no movement. Cautiously, then, he skirted the new lake and started to clamber up the long slope. Three miles above he found a side draw and turned up it. He had no intention of staying to be trapped when Laws' riders returned to search for their employer.

CHAPTER FIFTEEN

THREE DAYS LATER Boyd Reynolds reached the railroad. He had walked the full distance, most of it through the hills, all of it at night. He had no idea of the whereabouts of Jud's crew and no desire to meet them. A rabbit he shot had been his only food.

He entered the outskirts of the town an hour after darkness, walking past the cattle pens, noting with satisfaction that the TC cows were still held there. Then he headed for the sheriff's office.

The sheriff had known Boyd's father. He sent his deputy for the doctor and for food and coffee. He listened grimly to Boyd's report.

"I talked to Miss Carstairs and Jenny Hay when they first got here. We impounded the herd when it came in, and I sent a posse out looking for you and Jud Laws. They got back this evening. They'd found some of Laws' men who told them Jud was dead and claimed they didn't know where you were."

"I didn't want them to know," Boyd said. "Are they around?"

The sheriff's smile was thin. "They rode out of the country. They seemed in a hurry to leave."

The doctor came, shaking his head at the inflamed hand. "If you weren't as healthy as a horse you'd lose that," he said.

He cut away the proud flesh, cauterized the wound and replaced the broken stitches. Reynolds sat rigid, white-faced, his lower lip clenched between his teeth.

"Hurt a little?" the doctor said gently.

"After what I've been through this last week nothing hurts very much."

The sheriff brought a bottle of whiskey. "You want Laws' men picked up?"

Reynolds shrugged. "We can't prove which of them killed my men. Let them go as long as they stay away from Hunt Valley."

He had two stiff drinks and some food. Feeling better, he thanked them and turned toward the hotel. The girls, the clerk said, were in room ten, and he climbed the stairs and knocked at the door.

Belle Carstairs opened it. She stood staring, gasping, until astonishment subsided and she threw her arms around his neck, kissing him wildly. "Boyd. Oh, Boyd. We thought you were surely dead." She pulled him after her into the room. "Look at you—so thin, so white. Are you all right?"

"Fine," he said, but was glad to settle into a chair. "The sheriff says the cattle buyer will be in from Denver tomorrow. We'd better get a pickup crew and cut the pens for the stock and young bulls. You can't just leave the range empty."

"You take care of it. You're the TC manager, remember."

He glanced at Jenny, standing beside the open door. "What shape are you in?"

"I'm all right." They were her first words, tightly contained.

He looked back to the English girl. "Cleaver and Laws are both dead. The balance of your cattle are on a ranch they started in Wyoming. We'll get the best lawyer in Cheyenne, but I don't think we'll have any real trouble recovering the critters. Even if the brands are vented, there are no bills of sale. But it's going to take months, maybe years to straighten out the mess Laws made of the valley."

"It's your job," she said. "I wouldn't know what to do."

He nodded. "I'll need your power of attorney."

"You can have it, but I'm going to stay here to help."

He looked at her, seeing the heightened color in her cheeks, then he turned to speak to Jenny. The doorway was empty.

"Where's Jenny?"

126

"Probably gone to her room. It's number five, but—"

He was already on his feet. "I'll see you in a while." He did not wait to hear her answer, but hastened to knock on the door of room five. There was no response. He tried the knob. It was unlocked. And the room was empty. He stood puzzled, then turned quickly toward the stairs.

To the clerk he said, "Miss Hay, did she leave just now?" The man nodded.

"Where did she go?"

"Home, I guess. She had no money and said to send the bill to Kernville."

Boyd hurried from the hotel, heading for the livery stable. Jenny was in the office, waiting as the hostler saddled the horse. She turned as Reynolds came in, and her face blanched.

He said anxiously, "Where are you going?"

"Home." Her voice was unsteady.

"Tonight? Why?"

"I only waited until I knew you were safe."

"But what's the hurry?"

"I've got to get back. I'll have to straighten things up. I'm—I'm leaving the country."

"Leaving?" His amazement was growing. "What kind of nonsense is this?"

"It isn't nonsense." Her voice had sharpened. "I can't run the hotel without Father. I'll have to make a living somehow. I'd just be in the way here."

"What are you talking about?"

"Boyd," she said, "listen to me and try to understand how I feel. I used to have a schoolgirl crush on you, but when you came back I realized it was not a crush." She flushed deeply. "I even let myself hope, for a little while— and then Belle Carstairs arrived. Yesterday she told me how she felt about you, that she'd never met a man until she met you. She said she would even live in this country because of you. I'm sorry. I hope you will be very happy. But I simply can't stay and watch it, I—"

The hostler opened the door. "Your horse—" He stopped.

Boyd Reynolds had the girl in his arms. Boyd was say-

127

ing, "You little fool. Won't you even give me the chance to decide who I want to marry? Stop making up my mind for me. That's no way for a wife to behave."

Then he was kissing her, thoroughly, and both of them were unaware that they had a witness.

The End